his long shot

A LOVE GAMES NOVEL
by
ALLYSON LINDT

For my eternal dragon

chapter one

Rae pressed her forehead to her sister's apartment door. The coffee she'd grabbed before she caught her connecting flight two hours ago was a distant memory, and the exhaustion of spending half her day traveling filled her bones.

But she was here now and looking forward to spending some time with Chloe, catching up with the rest of her family, and friends. Just being back in her hometown.

She pulled her phone from her purse and dialed.

"Sis, hey. I'm so sorry; I meant to call." Chloe's greeting was cheerful despite the fatigue in her voice. "Did you land?"

Poor kid must be working late. Though *kid* wasn't really appropriate anymore. Chloe was only five years younger than her twenty-eight. Rae pushed sympathy into her tone. "About an hour ago. You sound swamped."

"A little. We're trying to get a demo together for E3, and QA found a bunch of last minute crap."

Chloe's tendency to slide into industry lingo could be difficult to follow. Fortunately, this time Rae kept up. E3 was a huge annual video game expo, and QA was quality assurance—the group responsible for testing the games Chloe and her colleagues created. "It's no big deal. I'll grab dinner and meet you back here. How long do you think you'll be?"

If she were visiting any other city, Rae would have found an apartment, or at least an extended stay motel. That was for work though, and this was a vacation combined with looking for her next contract. Chloe offered her guest bedroom for Rae's use while she was in town, and it sounded a lot more comfortable than a generic room with no personality.

"I don't know how late we'll be here." Chloe's sigh echoed off the mic. "Stop by and grab a key from me, so you can at least get settled."

"Umm…" Rae didn't want to hesitate. She shouldn't care who else may or may not be in the office. Even if her sister's boss was Rae's high school sweetheart.

A sliver of doubt lingered in her head and squeezed her heart. Each memory sent a new spark or tremor racing through her veins. His steel-blue eyes that seemed to reach into her soul and pluck out the important pieces. Hungry kisses stolen in the front seat of his car, parked in front of her parent's house late at night. Hours spent talking about everything under the sun. More kisses.

She pushed the images aside. Ignoring her racing pulse wasn't so simple.

"You can't avoid him forever," Chloe said.

But they were going on ten years, and that was a decent run. Chloe was right. A decade was a bit ridiculous. "I'm not avoiding anyone."

"Glad to hear it." Some of the weariness in Chloe's tone vanished. "Stop by, grab my keys."

"I'll be there in twenty minutes." At least it was a gorgeous evening. After Rae made her way back to her rental car, she headed downtown. She'd visited Chloe's workplace a few times in the past. The drive would be pleasant. It was after five on a Friday afternoon, so traffic was heading in the other direction, and if she was going to be downtown anyway, she could pick up dinner. See what was new.

A jolt of longing sped through her. At times, it felt like it was all new. With more time between each trip home, the city had a chance to remake itself over and over. That wasn't really the case, but it felt like it.

She loved her career, and the fact she got to see the country, a new city every six months to a year. However, watching a place change, and coming back to it already grown were two different experiences. Sometimes she had the desire to find a place to call home base, and not have to pick up and go again just as she got comfortable. That urge usually hit right about the time she spent too long out of work, which meant she needed to remember this was a vacation, not a place to grow roots.

The buildings grew taller and closer together as she traveled nearer to the center of Salt Lake City. Nothing comparable to the large skyscrapers on the East Coast, but the older architecture here was gorgeous. Granite three- and four-story buildings sprawled with arched windows, and columns holding everything together.

Rae parked near a cluster of the century-old

structures and made her way to one in the middle. She skipped the elevator—classic or not, the jerky ride scared her—and took the narrow stairs to the second floor. The etched glass on the only door in the hallway proclaimed *Cord, Incorporated*.

She cringed at the brown paper taped to the glass hiding something. A chemical scent singed her sinuses. Was it being updated to add *A Digital Media Company*? She pushed inside and paused at the empty reception desk. No one was going to mind if she wandered back to Chloe's workstation. She knew the way.

Her earlier hesitation fluttered again, bringing her to a standstill. If Zach was here… She shoved against the thought with all her might. Chloe was right. It wasn't as if they could avoid each other forever, and there was no way he still cared what happened all those years ago.

Did Rae care? Sure she kept up on the trade magazines that featured him. That was how she knew he still looked incredible. But that was because her sister worked her. One of her closest friends was his business partner.

What had started as all those years ago as irritation and a feeling of betrayal for the way they left things, became habit as time passed. An instinct to keep him out of her life, because that was just what she did.

"Rae?" A familiar voice tickled her ears.

She grinned as she spun toward the sound. She hadn't kept in touch with many people from high school, but Scott was the one person she could geek out with. They'd been each other's confidants and anchors to sanity. He was also CTO—Chief Technology Officer—and co-founder of Cord.

True, last time they'd seen each other in person, almost three years ago, things were awkward. Their conversations since had grown shorter and farther apart. But he was still Scott.

When he wrapped her in a friendly hug, her trepidation faded. "Hey." She threw her arms around his neck.

He squeezed tight, lifting her off her feet, before letting go. "You look good. I wish I'd known you were going to be in town."

"Last minute plans. My next contract fell through, so I thought *impromptu vacation*." She took a few steps back, so she didn't have to tilt her head quite as much to see him. He looked good too. Then again, he always did. Almost a foot taller than her five feet four, with broad shoulders and a flat stomach, he defied everything about the geek stereotype… Until he talked tech.

He designed Cord's graphics engine and so many other bits of underlying code for their games. When he got going on a brainstorming tangent, his ideas flew over a lot of heads.

"If you're here for Chloe, I'm sorry, but I need her working tonight. No exceptions, even for you."

The stilted transition from friendly to business both relieved and disappointed her. She missed the friendly banter with Scott, but what if the last time they got together was her warning they couldn't get that level of closeness back?

"She told me. I'm just borrowing a house key." Rae wasn't surprised Chloe hadn't mentioned the trip to her coworkers. When Chloe landed the head writer job a few years back, she and Scott left any conversation about Rae off the table, especially at work. Chloe earned the position on her own merits and wanted people to know it, instead of thinking her older sister pulled strings with the boss.

Scott rested a hand at the small of her back and pointed her toward the conference and meeting areas. "They're all in the war room."

Concern brought back the foul taste the new glass etching had left in her mouth. Almost a year ago, Cord had been subject to what Chloe referred to as a *no-lube violation*. Rae interpreted that to mean a *hostile takeover* by Digital Media.

Things had been all hands off from the new parent company until just a few months ago when they started to sink their claws in. "Is it that bad?" Rae asked.

"I'm stealing my people's Friday night. What do you think?"

"Chloe's version is the world is going to explode in the fiery death hate of DM. Give me some substance."

Scott raked his fingers through his hair. "One of their top executives is going to be in the office *interviewing* everyone to see who's vital to the group, and they've upped our E3 delivery from a video to a fifteen-minute playable demo."

Translation—staff cuts on top of extra work, plus babysitting upper management. "Ouch."

"Yup." Scott steered her toward an open door emanating an eerie atmosphere. Not even whispered conversations interrupted the clack of fingers on keyboards. Tension hung in the room and no one looked up from their computers.

Seven people sat at a round table that almost filled the room. Cables and laptops ran to every outlet, and empty pizza boxes were piled in the corner, with one still sitting in the middle of the group. The building cleaning staff must have been by recently, or the trash would be overflowing with Mountain Dew cans.

Despite the almost tangible stress and the mess, the setting energized Rae. She loved what she did for a living, but if she could spin her skills into landing something like a director of finance position for a video game company, she'd take it in an instant. Too bad jobs like that were few and far between.

Rae recognized some of the bowed heads, worshiping the gods of overtime. Jordan—Chloe's boyfriend and Cord's head of art and character design—sat at the far side of room, the largest screen almost blocking him from view. Chloe was next to him, pen in her mouth, brow furrowed. The fact Rae and Chloe were sisters would have been more obvious, but Chloe dyed her hair black and loved her heavy eyeliner, which made her fair skin appear even paler. Unlike Rae who didn't work to hide her dirty-blond hair or avoid the sun at all costs.

Rae's traveling gaze skittered to a stop when she saw *him*. Butterflies whirred to life in her chest, and her heart skipped a beat. Zach, bent at the waist, arm on the back of a developer's chair, pointed at something.

The recent cover of *Forbes* hadn't done Zach justice. Blond hair pulled into a ponytail hung just past his collar and perfectly pressed slacks and a button-down shirt covered a slender, sturdy frame. He looked better than he should. Seeing him again, even after so long, summoned more fond memories. The way they could spend hours, and weekends, and holidays together, and still never tire of each other. She resisted the urge to shake her head to rid herself of the past.

"Look who I found." Scott's announcement sounded unnaturally loud. Several people jumped, and everyone turned toward them. Except Jordan, headphones on, volume apparently cranked up.

Zach's gaze met Rae's for the briefest second, and her breath caught. Something unreadable flashed across his face—surprise? Hope? Irritation? Just as quickly, a neutral smile appeared, and he turned back to the developer.

"You made it." Chloe bounded from her chair and crossed the room. She hugged Rae then pressed a key into her palm. "I'm really sorry. Make yourself at home. Keep in mind there's probably nothing but Dew in the fridge, and with any luck, the head slave drivers won't keep us here too late." She turned to Scott. "Kidding, of course."

"Of course." He sounded more amused than annoyed.

Chloe returned to her seat and nudged Jordan, who looked up long enough to wave. Rae exchanged a few more hellos, including a polite hi directed at Zach. With a promise to Scott they'd catch up when he was only neck-deep in work instead of in over his head, she turned away.

She only made it a few steps, when Scott's call

made her pause.

"Rae, wait up."

She whirled back to face him, and her gaze landed on Zach. He watched them, curiosity in his eyes. Rae pulled her attention away first, not wanting to read too much into his expression. "What's up?" she asked Scott.

"How have you been?"

The question was polite enough. Friendly conversation, a kind inquiry. But it was such a benign greeting compared to the bear hug, and a sharp contrast to the business demeanor, that it made her frown. "I've been okay. Working, living, seeing the world." She would have turned it back on him, but she had a pretty good idea, at least on the surface, how he was.

"Are you going to be in town long enough we can actually catch up, instead of this superficial bullshit?"

Her smile returned full-force. That was the Scott she knew. The man she missed. "I have a feeling my schedule is more open than yours. What'd you have in mind?"

"We do breakfast Sunday mornings. Brunch, more like it. We're thinking Silver Lake up in Park City this weekend. Join us."

"Us." She wasn't asking, she already knew he meant Zach.

"Not an answer." Scott reached for her hand, and squeezed her fingers. "Does it even matter anymore?"

Why did people keep asking her that today? No one cared before now. Or maybe everyone always had, and it was time for her to grow up and move on. "I don't want to interrupt your plans, but if you're both okay with it, it sounds great."

"Excuse me." A male voice interrupted from behind.

She turned, and found herself face to face with a FedEx delivery guy. She jumped in surprise. Her hand flew to her hammering heart, and she choked on a nervous laugh.

The man glanced up from his clipboard, and handed Scott an envelope. "This one's for you specifically."

Scott took the letter, jaw clenched.

"See you around." The man's voice trailed off as he headed back to his truck.

"First name basis with the FedEx guy?" Rae teased, more because she wasn't sure what else to do than because the situation called for it. "You really do make it a point to know everyone."

Scott blinked and shook his head. "Something like that. I need to get back to my office." His voice was quiet, gaze never leaving the envelope as he flipped it over and over in his hands.

"Yeah." She didn't think he heard her. She had no idea what was in the letter, or if he even knew, but whatever it was drowned out any remaining catch-up time tonight. She shuffled back to the parking garage, the random invitation and the anti-climactic potential to end a grudge she'd carried too long, replaying in her head. *Weirdest start ever to a vacation.*

chapter two

Zach leaned back against his desk, palms resting on the mahogany behind him, fingers drumming on the lip. All things considered, he'd rather wade through an awkward conversation with Rae than face his company's mortality. It hadn't even been a decade since he and Scott founded Cord.

Rae was a big name these days. The woman companies called when they needed to recoup their losses without drastic means like bankruptcy or tax evasion. And, he wasn't complaining about the white top she'd worn, fabric just sheer enough to know she had a turquoise bra underneath.

Fuck, who was he kidding? It took more will power than he thought he had to not stare the entire time she was here. Everything about her was *more* than he remembered. More confidence. More maturity. More polish.

More desire spilling under his skin.

"Are you listening?" Scott's question cut through the drifting thoughts.

Zach forced his attention back to his best friend and business partner. It didn't matter if he heard. The conversation hadn't changed much since they lost

Cord in the hostile takeover ten months ago.

Scott nodded at something behind Zach. "It's always good to see her again."

It was nice. Fantasy sideswiped Zach's thoughts and slid in to take their place. The same images that taunted him the moment she stepped into the war room. Rae's teasing laughter growing heavy as he backed her against the wall, her gasp as he peeled off her thin top. That playful lick of her lips she'd had talking to Scott. The one she probably wasn't even aware of.

The teasing heat inside cranked toward scalding. "I guess. You'd know better than me."

Scott raised an eyebrow. "Right." He looked at the piece of paper in front of him. "This changes everything."

And they were talking about the letter again. Zach exhaled slowly. "I know." It didn't really. *It* was a formal copy of the offer Digital Media was making to buy Zach and Scott out of their Cord company shares. They'd known it was coming for a while now. New management rarely wanted to keep the old guys around in any capacity, let alone a leadership role.

Scott hopped from his seat, and paced the length of the office. "So what do we do?"

The specifics had varied over the past few months, but the meaning of the conversation never changed. Neither of them wanted to accept they were out of options.

He hated the entire situation—he put as much time into building Cord as Scott had—but as of now, denial was no longer an option. "Call our favorite headhunters and see if anyone else is hiring executives."

"This isn't a joke." Scott's flat tone matched his expression.

There was a list to pick from of what came next in the conversation. Zach and Scott each had their own favorite ways to pretend things weren't so bad, and he'd narrowed down the most likely option for Scott this evening.

This would be the negotiation. Couldn't they just stay on long enough to launch their current game? DM would have to keep them around after that if they did a great job. They just had to prove they could play nice with their new owner.

Like trained dogs on a leash.

Scott stopped and faced him, dark eyes narrowed.

Or maybe it would be the *Can we pretend we never saw this?* argument.

"Is this what you wanted?" Scott asked.

Zach choked on a canned response. He didn't like being caught off-guard. "Excuse me?"

"This isn't just our lifeblood; it's our dream. It's being ripped away, and you're making jokes about talking to recruiters."

Irritation snaked through Zach's veins. Usually he'd temper his answer. Business meetings: he'd filter his thoughts. Dinner with colleagues: he'd tone down his response. There was no need for any of that with Scott "It was a fucking hostile takeover. It sucks. What do you want me to do?"

Scott clenched his jaw and his nostrils flared. "Maybe that's what you were hoping for. Maybe that's why you opened us up to it in the first place."

Every word dug deeper, and the heat in Zach's veins turned to fury. It'd been months since they had this argument, and he was never in the fucking mood.

"Wait, I've got this one. Let me guess. *You're the one who begged me to let Kelly invest. I think part of you wanted this.*" He let the snideness slide into his voice as he mimicked Scott. It was easier than focusing on the betrayal that thudded behind his ribs every time he thought about *her*.

Scott squared his shoulders. "If you know what I'm going to say next, tell me I'm wrong."

"Because that worked so well for me the five billion other times I did so." Zach hated what happened with Kelly. Nothing about the situation was good. Five years ago, he and Scott had been struggling to bring this company to life.

Kelly and Zach had been together since just after high school. They loved each other. *Love*, Zach almost gagged on the word. He was an idiot for thinking something like that was real. But at the time, he bought into the delusion.

She offered to invest her family's money, to keep them afloat. They just had to make her an equal partner. The decision made them the company they were today—an organization worth buying out.

A year ago, Zach proposed to her at E3. It was going to be big. *Huge*. A media stunt that would keep their company name in the headlines for weeks.

And it had. Kelly found out about the proposal beforehand and made arrangements to sell her company shares minutes before the market closed. As she was ditching a controlling share, she was also turning Zach down in front of hundreds of cameras.

The video of her rejection went viral, along with the news she'd dumped her part of the company. Their stock was worthless within twenty-four hours.

Zach's fingers twitched over the pack of smokes in his shirt pocket. He swallowed a few breaths of air to try to sate the craving. It didn't squelch the rage and hurt.

"We would have found a way without her," Scott said.

Zach refused to play the *what if* game. "The only reason you didn't want Kelly's money then was—" He snapped his jaw shut before he could add *because she didn't love you*. He was pissed off, but he wouldn't cross that line.

Fuck if he wanted to, though. Months of impotence and frustration, banging their heads against the wall with new management, were all culminating in this. Zach clung to the last threads of civility that he had, but one by one, they were snapping.

"I would rather have failed than owe her anything." Scott spat the retort.

Zach exhaled through clenched teeth. "Funny, that's not what you said back then. Besides, can you fathom not being here right now? I'm not talking about today. You would have walked away from *your* dream to spite a potential investor?"

"It wouldn't have been spite."

"You would have taken money from anyone else." They'd been desperate. Hungry. Driven.

"I didn't take it from Dad. I said *yes* because you wanted it."

"Nope. That's bullshit of the highest grade, and you know it." Zach clipped off the disagreement. He owned his mistakes, but this wasn't one of them. The company was Scott's idea. His dream.

"Fine." Scott threw his hands up before he started pacing again. "No one did anything wrong. This is all just an unhappy coincidence."

It was definitely Kelly's fault. There was no doubt there. Blame could be cast all over the place, but she'd lied. She'd manipulated. She'd violated their trust.

And broke my heart.

Right. That.

"At least you learned your lesson before it was too late." Sarcasm hung heavy in Scott's sneer. "Oh wait, no you didn't. Maybe it's a good thing we lost everything. Otherwise you might have signed over controlling interest to the next piece of ass who came along."

Zach's fury erupted. "*Fuck you.*" His raised voice bounced back at him. "Kelly wasn't just some random one-night fling. Mistake or not, I thought I loved her. I thought she loved me."

He'd been wrong on both counts.

Just like with Rae.

No. Kelly was different, and this wasn't the time for that tangent.

The tension faded from Scott's frame, and his shoulders slumped. That was one thing about Scott— he had a short fuse, but it burned out as quickly as it ignited. "I know. This isn't on you, or me. It bites pretty hardcore, though."

"And rehashing this doesn't give us any

answers." Zach scrubbed his face. His anger didn't dissipate so easily, but he'd stash it in tight muscles and tense joints until he was along.

"We'll have to look harder."

They'd need a quantum microscope to peer any deeper for solutions than they already had. If he dove back into the heated words, he wouldn't be able to rein his temper in again. "Right."

"I invited her to breakfast with us."

Kelly? No. Rae. The tension in Zach's neck cranked past painful. "Why?"

"Because the two of you can't do this forever. Because…I'd rather see you talking than not, and at least this, I have control over. Anyway." Scott raked his fingers through his hair, the brown spikes bouncing back into place the moment he dropped his hand. "Let's call it a night for everyone. Go get dinner."

"Good call." Zach could smoke on the drive there. Crank the music. Scream out some of this frustration.

By the time they got to the restaurant, he'd be in the mood to bullshit with Scott like normal. And maybe the waitress would be cute. Short. Curvy. Financial genius who'd made a name for herself saving dying corporations—

Nope. That probably wouldn't be their waitress. Why the fuck was Rae back in his thoughts? He'd seen her across the room and exchanged a terse greeting with her.

But she looked good. She sounded incredible. And kisses from a decade ago lingered on his lips with her name.

"I'm going to send everyone home." Scott hovered near the door, resignation and disappointment peppering his words. "Meet you downstairs?"

"Yeah." Zach headed for the stairs. His footsteps echoed against the concrete of the stairwell, hammering with the chaos of this thoughts. He made it about halfway down before the carefully constructed dam around his emotions burst. The weight hit him full force, stealing his breath and forcing his frustration out in a drawn-out scream. *"Fuuuuuuuck!"*

chapter three

Rae followed the winding mountain road toward Deer Valley, about twenty-five miles east of Salt Lake. When she was younger, she couldn't wait to get out this state. Utah was too small. Too…nowhere.

Now the green lining the hills, the trees, and the light traffic helped soothe her racing thoughts. It was more pleasant to focus on the wood-faced businesses that were a city requirement to make the place look rustic, than the broken record of a question *What do I say to Zach?*

Letting him into her head dragged back memories of the last time she'd been up here. A sharp pain grew in her chest.

It was their senior year of high school. She and Zach put in a brief appearance at the Valentine's Day dance. He didn't seem disappointed when she begged off early. Her shoes dug into her feet, and blisters formed faster than she thought possible.

He'd led her out to the car, and slipped her heels off. Told her she hadn't needed the miniature torture devices, she looked gorgeous either way.

The sweetness in his gestures then tugged at emotions she'd locked away long ago. A lump grew in her throat at the vivid surge of feelings, and images that blended then with now.

He hadn't been ready to go home—he rarely was, and Rae never complained. Any excuse to spend more time together was fine with her.

The drive brought them up here, then to a small clearing surrounded by trees. In February, snow covered most of the ground, and no one plowed the back roads, so they were safe from prying eyes.

That night, they spent hours talking, the way they always did. Moving into the back seat of his car so they could cuddle. Turning the car on long enough to get warm every time the chill seeped in. Making out. Losing her virginity. Saying they loved each other.

His voice from the past gripped her lungs like a vice, and she gasped. It had been amazing back then, but never better than that night. The same night it started to fall apart. The night he started assuming their future would be one way, and ignoring her opinion about wanting something else.

She pushed the bittersweet surge aside, and focused her attention on the scenery and the rest of her drive. A few minutes later, she pulled into the Silver Lake Lodge parking lot. She smiled at the black SUV in a spot near the entrance. She hadn't seen Scott's newest ride, but he'd had the G4M3G0D vanity plates longer than the Escalade.

Since he wasn't waiting outside, she headed into the restaurant. Scott and Zach already sat at a table on the back deck, overlooking the lake. A glance at her phone told her she was five minutes early.

She watched them through the glass as she

approached. Scott wore jeans, battered high tops, and a faded black concert T-shirt. Looking at him, there was no indication the man was worth millions.

Zach was his opposite. Polished cotton button-down, trousers, and an etched on smile as he leaned in and said something to their waitress, drawing a laugh from her. And he still looked amazing.

Heat raced across her skin, drawing her senses to life, and she was pretty sure the sun didn't cause it. Rae forced her gaze away, and pushed the door open to step outside and join them. Both heads swiveled in her direction. The waitress tucked her notebook in her apron pocket and brushed by Rae.

Zach and Scott both stood as she approached, and Scott greeted her with a hug. Zach's smile still didn't reach his eyes as he shook her hand. The entire situation cranked her nerves in opposing directions. It was the wrong kind of appropriate. Casual, but forced.

"I'm sorry if I kept you waiting." She added a sweet smile to her apology. It was easier than acknowledging the reality of the situation. The men arrived to any business meeting fifteen minutes early. It gave them time to collect themselves before things started. At least one of them didn't see this as a casual breakfast with an old friend.

Did she expect anything less? She had no idea how to react to Zach. There was a tug of ambivalence that he was doing the same with her.

"You're right on time." Scott held out her chair, and scooted it in as she sat.

Scott and Zach both took their seats. The two played off each other's actions in a seamless ballet.

To do what they'd done though—making themselves a gaming industry megaforce—they needed an unparalleled synchronicity.

"You look good." Zach raked his gaze over her, lingering on her chest, before dragging his attention back to her face, and leaving goosebumps everywhere his eyes traveled.

Pretty, sincere words or obligatory ones? The teenager in her begged for it to be the former. Whispered in her head *maybe there's still something there.* The adult refused to listen. He was sexy as fuck to look at, and Zach now made for some good fantasies, but there could be no ties to what came before if she wanted to keep her sanity intact.

"Thanks." *Wow, this is awkward.* Or she was projecting. She was a professional with a solid career who bailed Fortune 500 companies out of bankruptcy. She could handle breakfast with her ex-boyfriend. Reassurances locked in place, she painted a mask into place. "So do you. You wear *CEO* well."

His chuckle was plastic. "Let's hope Digital Media's royalty agrees with you when they're in the office this week."

"I'm sure if they're reasonable, they'll see exactly what I see." Well, maybe not *exactly.* There was a missing gleam in his eyes when his smile was fake. She preferred that this morning. It was less distracting than the warmth she used to adore.

"*If they're reasonable* being the key modifier." Scott's laugh filled the patio. "I'm glad you still have a sense of humor."

She didn't mean it as a joke, but it *was* funny in a twisted kind of way.

Their waitress returned, set an iced tea in front of Zach, and coffee for Rae and Scott. She also placed a bowl of pink sweetener packets next to Rae. "He said you'd want a lot of this, and to keep the coffee coming."

Rae thanked her, then looked at Scott. He shrugged. "She didn't mean me."

"Has it changed?" Zach asked.

And that heat was back, rushing over her skin and teasing her senses. He still remembered how she took her coffee. "No. You were completely right."

"Are you ready to order?" The waitress asked.

"Give us a minute," Scott said.

"Actually—" Zach brushed her wrist without taking hold"—you can get me something."

The girl smiled and pulled out her notepad. "What's that?"

"Your number."

And like that, Rae's pleasant buzz plummeted into the new pit in her gut. He didn't order her coffee because he was lost in some sort of nostalgia. It was a polite gesture. The natural salesman in him shining through.

And she was fine with that.

The waitress scribbled something, tore out a sheet of paper, and handed it to Zach.

No surprise there.

Because Zach and Scott weren't just an unbeatable business team, they were two of the hottest bachelors out there.

Rae focused on mixing cream and sweetener into her coffee.

"Hey." Scott nudged her shoe with his. "Tell

him about the job you did with the cable company back east."

She shook her head. "No one wants to hear about my fangirl moments."

"I saw the financial write-ups on that." Zach's gaze fixed her as he leaned in. "They weren't even close to solvent before you got there. You were brilliant."

He followed her work? She ignored the flush of pleasure that tried to worm its way in. He was making conversation. Keeping things pleasant. "They weren't as bad as some of my clients. But I saved their asses." She didn't downplay her achievements in professional company, and wouldn't do it here, either.

"You really did. We were looking at them for streaming distribution at the time, and they were floundering." His knowledge had nothing to do with her, it was about the business.

The same way she followed Cord because of Chloe and Scott, not because it had anything to do with Zach.

Liar.

Her brain could shut the hell up now, thank you very much.

"Yeah, awesome. But we know she's amazing at her job." Scott tugged her fingers. "And you know that's not what I meant."

She did. Rae let a pleased smirk slide in.

Zach cocked his head to the side, studying her. "I have to know."

She waved her hand to brush off the attention. "I was auditing them, and they got me tickets and backstage access to one of their late night shows."

"You're leaving out the good parts," Scott said.

"Don't hold back on my account. I like your passion when you fangirl." Zach never looked away.

She rolled her eyes, but couldn't ignore the glow spreading through her. "Fine. One of their executives was showing me around, and Mister-I'm-important-because-I'm-on-TV was complaining to one of the directors. Bitching about the fact *some cunt was on set looking for an excuse to cut his budget, since advertising was down*. One of his guests that day was the guy from that vampire show. The blond one. Vampire guy refused to go on until the host apologized to me."

Zach's eyes grew wide. "No kidding. Nice."

"And…?" Scott prompted.

"And he took a few pictures with me, and was the kindest person imaginable the rest of the time I was in studio. About a week later, he sent signed photos of the entire cast to my office. Said no one deserved to be treated like that, especially for doing their job."

"Wow." Zach looked genuinely impressed. "Do you have a lot of stories like that?"

A few. "There aren't a lot of people clamoring to meet the accountant."

"So, you're going to be modest the rest of the day?" Scott asked.

She couldn't help her laugh. "Nah. Just for the next five or ten minutes."

"Right." Zach slid a little lower in his seat, his posture relaxing. That was a good look for him. Clinically speaking of course. "What's your favorite part of the job? Seeing the world on someone else's dime?"

Zach probably meant the question as a lighthearted segue into casual conversation. If he'd asked anything else, or at any other time, that would have been the result.

Instead, the suggestion spoke to the doubt that had nagged since her plane touched down. "Seeing new places all the time is nice. There are times I wish I had a permanent home."

Zach glanced away, fiddling with the spoon in his glass. "Maybe you should have thought of that before you walked away from that option."

And like that, the teasing mood evaporated. The underlying accusation in his words sliced deep, and she couldn't ignore what it exposed. "Passive aggressive doesn't suit you."

"I'd rather be direct." His cool, joyless smile slid back in. "Thing is, I'm sitting here waiting for an apology, or at least for you to acknowledge maybe, possibly, what you did could have been handled differently, and you're acting like the past doesn't exist."

An apology? From her? "Does it?"

"Are the two of you going to do this now?" Scott glared at Zach. "You can't even go one meal?"

Rae pushed her chair back. This was a mistake. All of it. She squeezed Scott's fingers. "I won't ruin your brunch. We'll catch up later."

"Fix this now." Scott grabbed her wrist, tight enough to let her know he was serious, but not so much she couldn't have broken free. "Ten years is too long, and I'm sick of it. Tell me you're not." He glanced between them.

A twist of her arm, and she'd be free. She could storm away from this conversation, leave her past in the dust a second time, and keep going on with life.

But it would keep coming up, as long as she and Zach ran in the same circles. Scott was right. It was time to actually put the past behind her, instead of shoving it into a box on the back shelf of her mind and pretending it didn't exist.

Rae scooted to the table again. She kept her gaze trained on Zach, and her voice even and cool. "I don't think it never happened, but I couldn't have moved on if I lost myself in what you did. What you expected. I can't apologize for wanting to live my life."

"You could apologize for making assumptions and overreacting." Zach mimicked her impassive tone.

"Excuse me?" The question came out harsher than she intended, but she let her indignation propel her words. "How is it possibly, in any universe, my fault?"

He narrowed his gaze. "How is it not?"

The edge to his tone scraped through her, leaving her insides raw. She stumbled through memories of the way they parted. The quiet irritation, the resignation as she walked away. "I'm not the one who was unreasonable. Didn't you just sit here and tell me you were impressed with what I've done with my career? And you think *I* made the mistake? What am I apologizing for?"

"The way you left." His reply carried an edge of huskiness. A hint she wasn't the only one rattled. But the way he leaned back in his seat was all a mask of confidence.

The memory that had hovered in the back of her head since she hit the canyon surged to the forefront. Both the good and bad bits of it. She wanted to match him fake smile for fake smile, but the past hurt too much. "You wanted me to give up everything, before I even got started with life, so I could stand by your side. How am I wrong for wanting otherwise?"

"I never said that. You assumed." There was no accusation in his reply.

She stumbled on his retort. That wasn't right. He was supposed to ask why he'd want anything else. To tell her she was silly for disagreeing. He was supposed to fuel the hurt. "What about all those long talks about how you pictured my future?" This had bubbled in the back of her head for years. "Your life plan to have two kids right out of college. To let me use my degree as a backup. For me to stay at home while you finished graduate school."

"I never said any of that." What was he playing at?

"Never directly. It was just in every single plan you ever made when you talked about *us*." Her own words dredged up more reminders. Those telling her they'd actually planned a future together at one point.

He winced. "You could have talked it through with me, instead of jumping to conclusions and running halfway across the country to avoid me." He leaned in to rest his arms on the table. His gaze softened. "It was supposed to be *our* plan. Not *mine*."

Why hadn't she ever heard this before? "You never—"

"I would have if you'd asked." Frustration and sincerity filtered through his response.

"Oh." She didn't know what else to say. He'd just taken a decade-old grudge and made her question every memory of the situation. The way he bounced rapid-fire from accusation to resignation left her head spinning.

Zach shook his head and pulled away. "I don't want this hanging between us. It's been too long."

"But then how would we make these weekend get-togethers awkward?" It took the last of her restraint to keep a joking tone in her question and the waver out.

He gave a short laugh. "I'm sure we can find a way."

Some of the tension faded, and she slouched in her chair, but they still hadn't resolved anything. Ten years of avoiding each other, and she wasn't the only guilty party there, and now everything was just supposed to be okay between them because they aired their grievances? She spun the conversation back through her head again, and realized neither one of them had apologized or accepted fault. "We can't gloss over this. That's what I did wrong before."

"And I'm not. You fucked up. I fucked up. I'm not putting this all on you, but I am asking you to stop and think for a moment. I'm swallowing my fucking pride to say that. Meet me halfway."

He made one point that shouted in the back of her mind in his voice. She'd left without ever talking it through with him. Walked away based on her own assumptions and fears.

But she hadn't imagined those conversations.

"Maybe, possibly, a little bit, I could have thought things through more clearly back then."

He raised an eyebrow. "Maybe?"

"Possibly."

"For what it's worth, I am sorry." His tone drew her gaze back up.

She managed a smile, and tried to ignore the catch in his voice that marred his apology. "Me too."

Zach loved that smile. He'd missed it. He also remembered it distinctly enough to know she still held something back.

He didn't have any intention of calling the waitress. He'd find her after and apologize. The media painted him as a billionaire playboy, and it was easy to keep up the façade. In reality, he was grateful work kept him too busy to date. After life with Kelly, he wasn't interested in any relationship—even a one-night version.

Zach asked for the girl's number to see if Rae flinched. Childish on his part, but years of dominating negotiations told him to always keep the other side on their toes.

Rae destroyed him when she left all those years ago. Never giving him a chance to make things right. The wound had scarred over, but never vanished.

He should be smug that he pushed her concession. Pleased that she yielded and gave him what he asked for.

It was a hollow victory, because it didn't change anything.

"Now that we're all friends again"—Scott

turned to Rae, no trace of tension in his voice—"you saw the new Iron Man, right?"

And like that, the lines on her forehead vanished, and her joy reached her eyes. "Opening night. The scene with all the drone suits? Didn't Layla fight a group like that last game?"

"Layla's fight was completely different and unique. Don't ever let Chloe hear you say otherwise."

Layla was the lead character in their game line, and Chloe was proud—rightfully so—of how she'd developed the character over time.

Rae turned her attention to her menu with the shake of her head. "That's why I asked you, not her."

"Then yeah, the two have a lot in common," Scott said.

Bonnie came back to take their orders, and gave Zach a tiny wave and giggle before she left. He definitely owed her an apology on their way out.

For now, Zach wanted to be more a part of this conversation. It was difficult to keep his gaze from drifting back to Rae, stilted apology or not. He needed a reason to focus on her that kept him from being creepy. "So you're still into vampires?"

"I'm a little picker these days about my bloodsuckers, but yeah." She searched his face, then gave her attention to her coffee.

Did she find what she was looking for?

"What is it that does it for you?" Zach was curious. She'd been a voracious reader in high school, and vampire novels were some of her favorites. He never understood the fascination though. "Is it the living forever thing?"

Scott shook his head. "It's the bloodsucking,

isn't it? You already said so."

"Eh, and eww. Gross." Rae scrunched up her face, squishing the freckles on her nose. That was adorable.

"Then it's the money. Gotta be. Hundreds of years old with a large collected fortune? That's sexy." Scott made it sound like the issue was closed.

Rae rolled her eyes, but the corners of her mouth quirked up. "Money he's probably stashed in a mattress somewhere to keep himself out of banking systems? God, it makes me twitch just thinking about it." She tucked her hair behind her ear.

Maybe finding an excuse to keep watching her was a bad idea. But Zach was enjoying the sight too much to change tactics. "It's the biting."

Pink flooded Rae's cheeks, and she ducked her head. She flicked her tongue over her bottom lip before catching it between her teeth. "It might just be. I mean, take Mr. Blond and sexy for instance— nipping along my neck, leaving that sharp sting that blends into pleasure…"

"That got personal fast," Scott said.

Zach didn't mind the new fantasies that teased him as a result. Biting Rae and hearing her sigh, then moan. Feeling the weight of her body press against him. She wasn't as reserved as she used to be.

Way back before the misunderstanding. Before she left. Years before he made an even bigger mistake with Kelly.

Rae was different than he remembered. Just as intelligent and compelling at her core, but more confident, and fuck if that wasn't sexy.

He'd changed too. He wasn't looking to fall into

a past mistake.

"Of course it's personal. You asked what *I* liked about them." Rae's retort was playful. "At least I'm not jerking off to—"

"Whoa. We don't talk about that." Scott held up a finger to silence her.

They were referring to a story Scott loved to tell in certain circles, about how he had to be unique as a kid. His first jerk-off material was the Lolth, the Queen Drow in the D&D Monster Compendium. "We do use it as blackmail material though."

The waitress returned with their food, but Zach was focused on the conversation.

Rae furrowed her brow. "How do you blackmail him about something brags about? Which, by the way, means you *do* talk about it."

Each time she licked her lips, or sipped her coffee, or fiddled with the neckline of her shirt, sparks raced across Zach's skin.

"I threaten to tell people he made it up." He was having fun with this. It had been a long time since a conversation was just simple and playful.

Scott nudged his plate aside and leaned in. "Can you imagine how much that would kill my geek cred?" he said in a conspiratorial stage whisper. "Booth babes eat up stories like that. Makes me all adorable and vulnerable and shit."

He and Zach both had the playboy reputations, but Scott lived his to the fullest. Zach couldn't keep up with the lifestyle. He'd tried the first few months after he and Kelly broke up, but it didn't work for him.

"Show them your high school football stats.

That'll crank your *geek cred* to about a billion," Rae teased.

This was so familiar. Like the last ten years had… not quite melted away, but wobbled a little. It was like it used to be.

Scott clutched his chest and feigned fainting. "Ouch. You wound me."

"No she didn't." Zach would think the words cruel in any other circumstance. But Scott hated playing football. He'd done it for his father, and left it behind without hesitation the instant he had the chance.

Scott grinned. "No. She didn't."

Rae nibbled on a piece of bacon. "Speaking of—"

"Booth babes?" Scott asked.

"Masturbation stories?" Zach shouldn't have said that. The words summoned a new wash of images. Rae putting on a private show. Gliding her hands over her body, making herself groan with pleasure while he watched.

She gave an exaggerated cough that didn't hide her amusement. "Conventions. Speaking of conventions. How was CES?"

"Are you using us for trade secrets?" Scott studied her warily.

Zach tugged her fingers playfully, to capture her attention. "Because if you're looking to use someone, I'll spill almost any secret under the right circumstances." Did he really say that? He didn't need to hook up with Rae.

But *fuck*, he wanted to.

"I really do just want to know how CES was."

Her blush spread down to her collar. It was so tempting to lean in and kiss the pink away. "I'm also trying to change the subject to something that doesn't have to do with Scott's penis."

"A phrase I hear far more than I expected in this line of work," Zach said.

Rae laughed, and traced a finger along the hint of bra strap that was peeking out from the shoulder of her top. The alluring combination of shy and bold was captivating.

"The booth babe was hot." Scott gave a stock answer. "Asked way too many questions about proprietary information, though."

"I get the point. I'll stop prying." Rae held up her hands in surrender. Amusement sparkled in her eyes.

"DreamHack was better." Zach answered honestly. The show was really more of a massive LAN party—to the tune of fifteen thousand or so people.

"Chloe was bummed she couldn't make that. I don't blame her. I've always wanted to visit Germany," Rae said.

Breakfast was probably cold at this point. Zach didn't care. The conversation was good, and the view was incredible. "I'm surprised there are places you haven't been."

"Not all of us are on the invite list for every electronics and video game trade show in the world." She didn't sound bitter. She almost sounded... regretful? "If you ever have an extra invitation..."

"You're first on my list." The offer came without thought. He could laugh it off as a joke, but he didn't want to take it back. He did want to gloss it over, though. Leave enough of a hint to let her know he meant it, without dwelling on the offer. "Out of all of the places you've been, if you had to pick one to settle down, where would it be? Both of you."

"Germany." It was probably good Scott knew without hesitation. He may have an opportunity to make it a reality soon.

But that was tied to the trouble with Cord, and Zach didn't want to dwell on that today.

"I don't know." Rae sighed. "I don't let myself think about it too much. Growing roots in my line of work is dangerous."

"But you have thought about it. You know the answer." Zach hadn't read her as well in the past as he did with most people, but he was right about this.

Sadness tinged her smile for the briefest second before vanishing. "It would be here."

Zach didn't know what to say to that. *After you spent so much time running away?* was definitely the wrong response. "Why here?"

"It's a place to come home to. It doesn't matter how many places I go, I'm drawn back here when I need to recharge." She shook her head, and focused on Zach. "What about you?"

"France. Italy. Maybe New Zealand." He should have put more thought into his answer before he asked the question.

Rae's entertained smile was back. "That's a big ambiguous for something *you* asked."

"I don't have a response. That's all there is to it." Getting away in general sounded good. Once he had the buy-out cash from DM, he could pick up and relocate. Spend six months in each place before moving on, until he found a spot that sang to him.

Scott nudged Rae with his elbow. "He's let his defenses down. He never admits when doesn't have an answer."

"Lucky me. What else can I ask you for while you're in a mood like this?" '

When she licked her lips like that? She could ask for anything she fucking wanted.

That was the wrong answer. He was looking, not touching. Or maybe touching a little, but nothing more.

Why was he even considering this? "You can't have the keys to the Porsche, no matter now much you beg."

Fuck. Now he was picturing her begging. Not that he imagined she pleaded for much of anything. But stripping her naked, laying her on the bed, and making her squirm under his attention… Hearing her whimper for release every time he pushed her to the edge of orgasm but not past…

"I'll have to ask for something else then." A hint of teasing seduction lingered in her voice.

He knew exactly what he wanted to ask her for. He couldn't pretend the attraction wasn't there.

One night. The two of them. Rewriting the ending to their relationship, and putting a pretty little bow on the entire thing, so he could move on.

It was a horrible, awful idea.

And he was going to figure out how to ask her without getting himself slapped.

chapter four

Rae plucked another walnut from her salad and nibbled on it. The weekend had been a nice break. After brunch almost imploding, she'd enjoyed the rest of the morning. It was good to hang out with Scott again, but Zach…

He caught her completely off-guard. She hadn't expected to have fun. To toe that line of flirting so closely that they almost obliterated it. She'd been reluctant to wrap things up, but she didn't have any illusions about the entire thing.

Zach was like so many executives she'd worked with over the years. Cocky, kind when it suited him, and he obviously had zero qualms about hitting on the waitress and Rae within a few minutes of each other.

Men like that could be dangerous. She'd had to ask a few to back off while she was on contract. When she first started doing this, the attention was flattering and the hookups that didn't violate ethical boundaries were fun. It didn't take long for her to figure out the sex was bad far more often than it was good. Most guys didn't care if she got off.

Even fewer were interested in anything that

came after the *wham bam*.

None of them were boyfriend material. That included Zach.

Monday had rolled around, and Chloe needed to go back to work this morning.

Rae couldn't put off looking for a new contract for much longer. She had savings, but she'd rather not dip into it if she could avoid it. She could job hunt and network from here since that all happened online and over the phone. Spend some more time with everyone. So she and Chloe were having lunch, to break up having to dive back headfirst into their Mondays.

"It's not a big deal," Rae said.

Chloe picked through the potato chips on her plate before plucking one from the pile. She was grilling Rae about whether or not she and Zach were on speaking terms. "Then you shouldn't have made it one."

"I didn't." In fact, she'd gone out of her way to avoid the topic this weekend. When Chloe asked how brunch went, Rae's answer was *fine*. It was simpler than trying to put words to her jumbled thoughts.

She thought she'd gotten away with it. Apparently Chloe's being back in the office revived the topic.

"Whatever." Chloe mumbled between bites of sandwich. She washed it down with a swallow of sweet tea. "So if you fuck him, will you ask him if I can have a raise?"

Rae laughed. "No."

"So you're thinking about fucking him."

Far more than she should be. For the last two

nights Zach had teased her dreams. "No."

"Right." Chloe waved at someone behind Rae.

Rae followed Chloe's gaze. What were the odds? Zach was there with Jordan, waving back from the counter.

Rae glared at Chloe. "Did you tell them we were going to be here?"

Chloe shrugged and grabbed another chip. "You mean did I say to my boyfriend *Meet us for lunch if you have a chance?* Besides, it's not a big deal. Right?"

"You're not as clever as you think you are." Rae kept the statement soft. She wasn't going to let this get to her.

"You love me, and you know it." Chloe's smirk spread into a friendly grin seconds later.

Jordan took the spot next to her, kissing her as he sat.

A hand rested on the back of Rae's chair, and a spark danced over her skin from the brief contact.

"Ladies." Zach's greeting was warm. "I was looking for one of you."

One of them?

"Oh?" Chloe sat up straighter.

Jordan stole one if her chips. "We're brainstorming commercial ideas."

"I didn't realize you were here with company. We can catch up later," Zach said.

It's all right. You can stay.

Stupid thoughts, betraying her desire for a drama free lunch.

Chloe nudged a chair out with her foot. "Eat with us. We're not the only ones who need to catch up, and we've got time."

"If you're offering…" Zach moved into sight.

I can put up with some drama for that view.

Yeah, she could. Besides, there didn't need to be drama. As long as she remembered this wasn't the Zach she'd been infatuated with. He was a good-looking guy with money and attitude. He knew it as well as she did.

Simple enough. "I'd love to hear the three of you talk shop."

"How was your Sunday?" Zach asked instead.

Chloe let out a heavy sigh. "*Someone* insisted I'd been working too hard, and *forced* me to eat ice cream and pizza while we binge-watched anime."

Rae smiled at the antics. "Guilty as charged."

"You'd better not have watched anything new." Jordan traced a finger along Chloe's exaggerated pout.

Chloe nipped his fingertip. "I did, but it's not my fault." Her attention was only on Jordan. "But it was epic, so I'll watch it with you again, and pretend I'm seeing it for the first time."

It was always sweet seeing them together. Chloe swore Jordan was the best thing to happen to her, even better than her job.

Rae agreed, the were good for and to each other. And now they were also lost in each other. Jordan was feeding Chloe potato chips.

"So it was a pretty good day?" Zach's question drew her attention.

Rae didn't mind the excuse to focus on him, while Chloe made googly eyes at her boyfriend. "It was fantastic. Do they ever get any work done?" She kept her tone playful as she nodded at her sister.

"We put them in separate parts of the office for a reason," he joked. "But seriously, she's one of those people who makes this whole endeavor possible." A frown whispered across his face, but vanished a heartbeat later.

Was the shift in mood to do with the DM takeover? Probably. "One of us had to inherit Dad's creativity." Rae wasn't being self-effacing—it was the truth. Their father was a novelist. Not the kind of name that made best seller lists, but he did well enough, consistently enough, to keep his family comfortable.

"You're kidding, right?" Zach looked at her in disbelief.

She frowned, despite his light tone.

"Rather, of course Chloe's brilliant." He drummed his fingers on the table near her arm, close enough she felt the whispers of heat. "But I'm talking about you. How far do you have to step outside the box, to bail out some of the places you save?"

Rae flushed at the implication. "It's not the same."

"It's not." Zach shook his head. "But it's still fucking creative."

"Plus, she writes some scorching fanfics," Chloe said.

Rae blushed. It would be nice if she could hide that. It gave her away every time, and it was running full-heat with Zach. She glanced across the table.. "I thought you two were off in your own world."

Jordan smirked. "Frequently. But never completely."

"Are there vampires in it?" Apparently Zach was stuck on the fanfic comment.

Rae couldn't ignore the tickle of satisfaction that he remembered their conversation Saturday. "No. It's um…" She shouldn't be embarrassed about it, but the writing wasn't something she did to be good. It was to keep her mind clear. Chloe only knew because Rae had asked her for feedback.

"It's Fruits Basket. And it's ninety-nine percent porn." Chloe offered.

Rae did a mental face-palm. "It's not." Like anyone would believe her now.

"No, it's not." Chloe relented. "But it *is* good."

Zach shifted in his seat enough to rest his knee against the outside of her thigh. Nothing obvious—it was a small table—but the contact sent desire racing along Rae's skin.

"Is that the one… where they turn into animals when someone of the opposite gender hugs them?" he asked.

Rae braced herself for teasing. "That's the one."

"How's that work then?" Zach sounded serious and looked captivated.

Maybe it was an act, but Rae was buying it. She wanted to revel in the attention.

"Very carefully," Chloe said.

Fuck, that made it sound bad. "It's not a bestiality thing. Cross my heart. The stories aren't about sex. And there's a lot of wickedness that can happen without two people ever touching."

Zach dipped his head near her ear and whispered, "I'd like to see that sometime." The heat of his breath raced over her skin. He straightened again. "The stories, I mean." His voice returned to normal.

Rea's response caught in her throat, stalled by her racing thoughts. How did he have this effect on her? Saturday. Now. He was just a guy. Flirty. Attractive. But like any other exec she ran into. None of that was enough to calm an imagination that wanted his attention to mean something more.

"Did you ask the cashier for her phone number today?" Oh, God. Why did she just say that? How bitchy was she? Could she take it back or laugh it off?

Zach raised an eyebrow. "No. That trick only works once, and it wasn't worth it last time."

What did that mean? Had he already gone out with the girl working the register? If this was anyone else, would Rae care? If he were any of these other men she compared his behavior to?

She wouldn't flinch. So why was Zach different? If this wasn't the same sweetheart of a boyfriend she had in high school, if he'd changed, did it matter how he acted?

As long as everything was consensual and no one misunderstood the relationship—or lack thereof—it didn't matter at all.

What if you're wrong? What if he is the same guy you love...d?

Wistful thinking got people hurt. She needed to ignore the bit of her stuck in that past. It wasn't fair to hold him to a higher bar because of what they'd had, if there was no future for them. He was free to live his life.

Why did it hurt to force herself to accept that?

"So, commercials." Chloe leaned in and shoved her plate aside. "TV, right? Since we need artwork?"

"Webisodes." Jordan's grin was just as big. "Five minutes long. Epic, right?"

Zach looked at Rae, the apology in his blue eyes masking something she couldn't interpret. "You sure you don't mind us talking shop?" he asked.

"She's fine," Chloe answered first.

"It's all good." Rae also wasn't complaining about the reprieve from her awkward question.

Besides, whether or not Zach was there, she loved listening to Chloe—or really anyone from their office—talk about what they were working on. Their jobs were so creative compared to the contracts she had.

The same *if-only* that had nagged her since Friday, about working for a gaming company long term, surged back. It wasn't an option, and she needed to let it go.

She focused on the conversation, which mostly consisted of Chloe and Jordan tossing story ideas back and forth, trying to make content work with visuals. Occasionally Zach would guide them in a direction. All three of their lunches went untouched.

"You can't do that." Zach interrupted as Chloe and Jordan reached an animated consensus on something. "It's too easy. She needs to work harder to solve the problem."

Chloe stopped, eyebrows reaching toward the top of her head. "Who's the writer here?"

Rae rested her arms on the table. "Of course they can do that. The idea is perfect for your target market. Layla has to rely on the hero at least a little."

Layla was the main character for Cord's top-selling title.

Zach shook his head. "Part of the point of this is to draw in new audiences. We have to step away from the sexist assumptions. Like that Layla can't defend herself."

Rae bit back her first response. It probably wasn't the right time to tell him he needed to start closer to the core of their company image—like its playboy executives—if he wanted to get rid of their sexist image. "She's already wearing skin-tight leather. It's not about toning her down or hiding her weaknesses; it's about making her confident and competent in spite of—and sometimes because of—those flaws. Self-reliance doesn't mean she has to do everything alone."

Zach studied her, eyebrow raised.

What was that supposed to mean?

"Besides." Jordan glanced at Chloe. "Self-confidence is sexy."

Zach exhaled loudly. "I'm not arguing that, but she's the one who has to save the day. She's the hero."

Rae was willing to concede that people didn't go to a *Wonder Woman* movie to see *Superman* save the day.

But *The Avengers* didn't protect the universe alone.

The Zach she knew back then understood that. Each person had to play to their strengths. The thought tugged threads of memory loose. Of late nights studying. Her coaxing him through math. Him walking her through vivid, vocal recreations of history, to help cement the details in her mind.

The cuddling, kissing, and unwinding after…

This wasn't the same man, any more than she was the same girl.

She considered her words before responding. "It's true, but she doesn't have to do it alone. Even Superman needs help sometimes, and you want her to appear human."

Chloe tapped her knife on the edge of her plate. "You're ruining my character. Layla is full-on control, even off screen."

Jordan smirked. "That's hot too."

Zach pinched the bridge of his nose, but the gesture didn't hide his faint smile.

"See?" Chloe looked smug. "He's our target market; he knows."

Zach leveled his gaze at her. "So are most of our developers."

Also know as a walking collective of dick and fart jokes wrapped in some hard-core testosterone. Rae shook her head. "If you're going to target it specifically to them, throw away any conversations about not being sexist, and just have her bounce around naked for five minutes. Besides," she said, looking at Chloe, "you're not unveiling her entire back story. You can leave things like what she does and doesn't dominate, outside of killing Legion, to the imagination."

Chloe's brow furrowed for a moment, before a small smile replaced it. "I suppose. That *is* what fan fiction is for."

The conversation moved in deeper, with everyone taking notes. Things finally wound down and everyone noticed their lunches again.

"Since when do you enjoy a good debate?" Zach asked Rae, when Chloe and Jordan were absorbed with each other again.

Rae couldn't place it exactly, but she had an idea where it started. "I learned it from watching you."

"At least you had a better teacher than money can buy." He winked.

What came next? Another suggestion about watching? Because each time that came up, her imagination jumped to overdrive. One thing that made Rae's blood race was being watched. There was a thrill to running her hands over her own body, touching all the right places, while a love looked on.

And the way Zach kept looking at her clothed, she wondered what it would be like to give him a private show.

She needed to talk to Zach, not stare at him and fantasize. "At least you're modest about it," she said with teasing sarcasm.

"No reason to hide when you're the best." The way Zach studied her, she almost swore he was talking about her. "But you already know that."

Rae did. She didn't land contracts by hiding what she was best at. In any interview, or even casual conversation, she could reel off a list of accomplishments. Hell, she could do it in her sleep. Right now the only thing she could think of was *I give a decent blow job.* "I try to save my boasting for the boardroom."

"What are you saving for the bedroom?" Chloe asked.

Rae could almost guarantee that her sister heard her just fine. "Nothing I'm going to discuss here." Though if the company were more private, if it was just Zach, would she?

She needed to decide right now if he was her ex-boyfriend, or just another sexy, playful twenty-something in an expensive suit. She was going with the latter.

Something inside withered and whimpered at the thought.

Zach knew why he'd been invited to lunch. He'd seen Chloe do this more than a dozen times since they hired her. She liked real life 'shipping, and apparently he and Rae were her latest matchmaking effort.

He wasn't complaining. He could have come up with a handful of ways to approach Rae outside of this, but Chloe's efforts made things go more smoothly.

Rae was more removed today than she had been Saturday, as though she was measuring her words more carefully. Was that because of him, or their other company?

He planned to remove the variables and find out.

"You know..." Chloe locked her attention on Rae, one corner of her mouth twitching up. "Friday night could have been a disaster if you hadn't been able to get a hold of me."

Zach was seizing this for all it was worth. A silly game. But until he had a chance to explain asking for the waitress's number didn't mean anything, Rae probably wouldn't hand hers over easily. "Maybe you should have called her and warned her," he said to Chloe.

Chloe made a half-snort, half-laugh noise. "Okay, whatever. My point is what if she needs to find me again and can't get a hold of me? Give her your number, so it won't happen again."

He'd bet money Rae had the numbers of about a quarter of the people in the office, including those Chloe actually hung out with after hours.

Rae looked at her sister in disbelief. "That doesn't even make any sen—"

"Good point. Give me your number." Zach unlocked his phone and handed it to her. Instinct twitched at giving the unprotected device to anyone, but even if he wasn't watching her, he'd trust her with it. How odd was that?

Rae worked her jaw up and down, then shook her head. She grabbed his phone, tapped the screen several times, then handed it back.

He glanced at the display. She'd entered her number under *Blonde with the Big Brain*. He looked back at her, to find that deceptively shy smile playing on her lips.

"Perfect." Zach grinned.

Chloe slid back into more random conversation with Jordan.

Zach wanted more time with Rae, but not here. Fortunately, now he had a way to change that. He typed out a quick message to Rae. *Had to check.* Make sure it was really her number. Not that he actually doubted, but it was a good ice breaker.

She grabbed her phone a second later, read the note, then looked at him. Her smile grew.

He typed *Can we talk?* and nodded at her hand as he hit *send*. This was childish. Passing-notes-in-class levels of immature. But it was fun and simple.

Rae's fingers twitched over her phone, but no reply came through.

What was she thinking? She shot him a questioning look.

Not quite what he'd hoped for. *After lunch? Away from other ears?*

She gave him a faint nod.

"If you have places you need to be, we won't be offended if you take off." Chloe interrupted the silent exchange.

He looked up to find her staring at his phone. He pocketed it with a smile. "I have to wait for the other party to be free anyway."

Rae let out a sigh so soft, no one would hear it but him.

Zach had misread Rae a few times since she arrived, but he was certain of one thing—she was interested.

That didn't mean what he was about to propose was a good idea, but he wasn't willing to back down until he knew for certain.

chapter five

After lunch, Rae told her sister she just wanted to duck in and say hi to Scott. She wasn't sure why she lied, but the flutter in her chest told her to keep this between her and Zach for now.

Her flip-flopping stomach made her grateful she didn't finish her salad. Zach emerged from his office just a few feet away, and she froze, heart slamming into her ribcage. He looked good. Better than good. *Delicious* might be a better word. He raised an eyebrow when he saw her.

She swallowed, not sure what to say. He was just the guy her friends worked with. It wasn't as if he mattered to her personally. The her of the past may have been madly in love with him, but current her had her own life, needs, and expectations. She wouldn't let a couple of winks and soft touches muddy the distinction between then and now.

You give him more leeway than you do anyone else.

Okay, maybe she'd let it all matter a little bit. An hour into resolving to treat him like any other schmuck, and she was already failing.

Not a bad thing.

Wasn't it?

He nodded toward his door, speaking before she could figure out what to say. "You have time now?"

"Sure." She let out a tiny breath—at least she kept her voice steady—and followed him.

He shut the door behind her. "For privacy. I hope that's okay."

She nodded and took the chair across from his desk. For as brilliant as his programmers were, they could be some of the most immature gossips and children when they found an excuse. Whatever this was about, she didn't need it to be their excuse.

What *was* this about?

"I like what you've done with the place." She studied the decor. It was actually as boring as the front lobby: straight out of a catalog, from the black leather chairs to the primary colored modern art decorating the walls. The only hint of personality was a single photo frame on the back part of his desk. Even in the half-angle view she recognized Scott and him with copies of their very first game.

"It does the job." Instead of sitting, he leaned back against the desk, legs extended and crossed at the ankles. It kept him less than a foot away.

She forced her gaze to his face. There was no reason to study the way his crossed arms accentuated a slender but firm chest. "So…"

"Something needs to change."

"You'll have to elaborate."

He drummed the fingers of his right hand on his left arm. "After all this time, I don't even know why we're holding on to any animosity."

She could point out they'd already gone

through this and apologized. Tell him it wasn't about animosity, because she didn't have the type of feelings for him that made her notice whether or not there was friction between them. A whisper of something less defiant pointed her in a different direction. He knew the air wasn't clear, regardless of what either of them said, and she'd been over him for years, so why were they masking old wounds trying to gouge them out at the same time? "You might have a point."

The corner of his mouth tugged up. "Did you just tell me I was right about something?"

Her apprehension mingled with light amusement. "Rumor is you're right about a lot of things."

"And we really can't avoid each other forever." He reached for the pack of cigarettes in his shirt pocket but dropped his hand at the last minute.

"Two successful meals hardly equals avoiding each other."

"Two in ten years."

She couldn't argue that. "It's a starting point."

"It is. Are you interested in a next step?"

A flicker of understanding blinked through her and vanished before she could grasp it, leaving a racing pulse in its wake. "Depends on what you have in mind."

"Neither of us ever got over the way we ended; we need closure. Rewrite the conclusion to that part of our lives, so it ends on a more positive note. One involving fewer clothes and less yelling. Though, some uncontained shouts of pleasure would be a nice bonus."

There was no way. *Arrogant asshole.* "You mean sex? Your idea of closure is sleeping together? After the whole *let's make amends* spiel, I expected better from you." If the idea bothered her so much, why did her skin heat and nipples harden at the thought? Because she liked the idea, just not his approach to asking.

He didn't need to know she had any reaction besides disbelief.

He raised an eyebrow. "I've played this out a couple times in my head, and I could beat around the bush a little more, but something tells me direct is the way to go. I can't not notice you. You're intelligent and gorgeous. You've grown up, filled out, and a reputation like yours? Fucking sexy. Not only that, but in person, you leave your reputation in the dust. I'm just saying we need to get this pent-up animosity out of our systems. Once we have closure, we can move on."

Fuck, he had a point. She'd rather he be blunt than wrap things in pretty words that could be misinterpreted. That got them in trouble last time.

She wasn't going to react to the compliments, despite the way they warmed her. She focused instead on the underlying insult. "Get it out of our systems. So charming. Why would you even think I'd do something like that?"

He rolled his eyes. "Okay, I'll bite. Yesterday at breakfast you said you're single. When was the last time you dated someone seriously?"

Two years ago. And even that wasn't really a relationship. "I don't know."

"Right. Last time you got off... with a partner?"

Three months ago—Vice President of Sales for a company she'd bailed out last year. Not that she had a type. "Not quite as long ago."

He shook his head. "Nice. More recently than the serious relationship?"

"You have work to do, and I need to be finding some." She stood to leave and strode toward the exit. He made it to the door before she did. Her heart slammed into her ribs at his nearness and determination, and she pulled up short.

She didn't replace the distance between them, torn between the familiar scent of peppermint gum and aftershave, and being furious about being blocked in.

"You're single, attractive, and married to your job. My money says you're not unfamiliar with the idea of a casual fling." He tugged on his ponytail. "Is the idea of being with me, no strings attached, as a way to rewrite our past, really that unappealing?" The cajoling vanished from his voice, replaced with something almost…sincere.

Yes. Yes. Yes. The answer chanted in her head. She needed to say yes. It might not be a big deal if it were anyone but him asking. "N-Obviously." She winced when her tongue betrayed her, stumbling over the lie.

He stepped out of the way and gestured to the door. "I don't believe you, but I'm also not a *no means yes* kind of guy. Sorry to take up your time."

Walk out the door, down the hall, to the stairs. That was all she had to do. Pretend this conversation never happened and go back to avoiding him. *So why am I still here?* "What about Scott?"

"You two aren't a thing, right?" He stared back, expression blank. "Because we don't usually share."

Share. The word twisted her thoughts into unrecognizable shapes. Why was she stalling? "No, we're not, and that's not what I meant."

His smirk was back. "We both know he doesn't like the tension. This gets rid of it."

Damn it, he was being logical, and part of her was intensely grateful for it. "One night. Just to give us a happier ending, and we move on?" What was she doing? He was treating her like a body with no brain. A means to get off and nothing more. Despite the compliments, this wasn't about getting to know her, it was about sex.

And what did you relegate him to during lunch?

That didn't stop the ache in her chest that Zach saw her the same way.

Hypocrite.

Maybe.

If he was smug about the fact she was still there, it didn't show on his face. "That's the idea."

Thoughts of running her hands over his sturdy chest, trailing her fingers down his arms, feeling his mouth…well…*everywhere*, made compelling arguments for giving it a try. And if this was about closure… She wouldn't mind putting the past behind them.

And once that tension was out of the way, maybe they could actually be around each other again without acting like children. Rediscover the friendship that existed before they dated.

Now you're just being delusional.

No. She was being an adult.

"Tell me what you're thinking." He hadn't moved, but his body seemed to go on alert.

No. No. No. Except it was exactly what she wanted. "If it clears the air and makes it possible for us to be in the same room…then yes."

"No other reason at all." He closed the distance between them and stopped close enough for her to feel his heat, but he didn't touch her. "It's all about closure." His attention lingered on her hips and again on her breasts. "Well, maybe not completely. I'll enjoy the view and the company."

Her breath hitched. His gaze seared her thoughts and made an ache of need throb between her legs. "When do we want to do this?" she asked.

He raised a hand until it hovered less than an inch from the side of her face, but never made contact. "What are your plans for this afternoon?"

"Now?" She almost choked on her question. Swallowing to clear her throat, she tried again. "You really know how to charm a girl, don't you?"

He searched her eyes. "You deserve to be romanced. Seduced. Even though it's only one time, you should enjoy it. As long as you promise that if I let you leave, I won't miss my chance." His voice was smooth. Assured.

You really won't. She'd like to think she was strong enough to write this entire conversation off once she walked out, but desire flowed through her veins, all of it inspired by the man in front of her. That didn't mean she had to let him know she was wavering. "It sounds like a wonderful setup, but it's not that simple. Rose petals and champagne don't erase animosity."

"No, but sometimes passion just needs to be redirected."

Passion. The word spiked her anticipation. Her body warred with reason every time he said something new. "Redirected like this?"

He reached behind him and locked the door. The audible click lit her nerve endings on fire with unspoken promise. He closed the remaining distance between them, and dipped his head. His lips hovered millimeters from hers, before he dove in and claimed her.

The sensation was so light, she wasn't sure she felt it. She leaned in, mouth opening, and a whimper escaped when he traced his tongue over her bottom lip. This didn't even begin to resemble resisting his suggestion, but her body craved more. Begged to find out what else lay buried under the kiss. His hand rested at the base of her neck, holding her in place. He deepened the kiss, going from gentle to hungry in an instant.

His tongue twisted around hers in a desperate dance, and desire blossomed in her gut. God, this was incredible. Had it been like this before? No, neither of them had been so experienced. She rested her hands on his chest, heat searing her palms. Dampness grew between her thighs, and her pulse tore through her body. It was familiar and entirely new at the same time. Safe and simultaneously terrifying.

She fumbled to find her breath when they finally broke apart. His finger caressed her swollen lips, dancing over the sensitive flesh.

"What are we doing?" She managed.

He nudged her back, hands on her hips, guiding

her until she bumped into the desk. His soft growl echoed in her ear as he kissed along her lobe. "Possibly the smartest fucking thing we've done in a decade."

He was as lost in the moment as she was. The realization made her slick with need.

Hands still on her hips, he lifted her to sit on the edge of the desk. She draped her arms over his shoulders, fingers interlocking at the base of his neck, and then pulled him in for another kiss.

His slacks scraped along her thighs when he forced her legs apart with his knee. Her denim skirt crept higher when he slid between her legs. She wanted him closer. Why were there so many clothes in the way? Nothing but a door stood between them and an office full of gawking and gossip, and she didn't care.

He traced a line with his lips across her jaw down to the base of her throat, and kissed the hollow immediately below her choker. His voice rumbled through her chest. "A collar. Fantastic."

"Don't read too much into it." A sigh cut off her laugh when he slid a hand under her shirt and up her spine. This wasn't the seduction he'd mentioned, but fuck it if that mattered. Her breasts ached to be touched. Her nipples pinched.

She scooted closer, wrapping her legs around his waist. The bulge of his cock behind fabric pressed against her mound, making her pulse scream in anticipation. What would it feel like to have him buried inside her?

Zach licked back up to her neck, then scraped his teeth along her shoulder, drawing a gasp. His nip was hard enough to sting, but not leave a mark.

A sharp knock echoed through the room, followed by Scott's insistent, "We need to talk."

Rae's already hammering heart almost tore from her chest. Disappointment crashed over her at the interruption. They broke apart, and she rested her forehead against Zach's chest. Her thoughts still ran rampant, and her nerves felt like electricity in a puddle. Frazzled but continuously sparking.

He dropped his chin onto the top of her head, and his quiet *fuck* echoed through her skull. "Figures." He stepped away.

"It's fine." Did she sound calm? *Damn it,* she didn't feel it. She hopped off the desk and straightened her clothes. If only she could as easily smooth over her soaring blood pressure. She ran her hands through her hair, even though he hadn't touched it, and dropped back into the chair. Her crossed legs didn't stifle the insistent need between them.

Zach closed his eyes, took a deep breath, and adjusted his slacks before unlocking and opening the door. "What's up?" His question was casual, any traces of his earlier growls gone as he let Scott in.

Rae twisted in her seat, arm draping over the back so she could watch the exchange. Did she look as calm as Zach? There was no way the torrent of emotions pouring through her was staying off her face. Would the flush of her lips show? At least she hadn't reapplied her lip-gloss after lunch. That would be smeared everywhere. Was her chest heaving as she searched for missing breaths?

Scott looked between the two, brow raised.

"Did I interrupt something?"

"Nope." Zach gestured to the empty seat next to Rae.

She failed to ignore the sting that flitted through her at the casual denial, but what did she expect? She certainly hadn't planned on telling anyone, and that was even if something *had* happened.

"Just trying to reach an agreement." Zach dropped into his own seat. "Playing nice, burying the hatchet, all that."

"I thought you already did that." Scott didn't sit. Instead, his footsteps carried him to the far side of the room before he spun on his heel and headed back toward the door. "Just got off the phone with Vance. They'll be in the office tomorrow instead of Wednesday."

One of the executives from Digital Media, and as Rae understood, about the foulest word anyone in the office could use. She rose, still squeezing her thighs together to suppress her body's pleading. "That's my cue." She couldn't bring herself to meet Zach's gaze. Instead, she looked at Scott. "Call me."

"Yeah." Scott sounded distracted.

After leaving Zach's office, she took the stairs as quickly as possible and then cut straight for the parking garage, not sure she could face anyone until she found more composure. What the hell had she been doing? Halfway to her car, her phone vibrated in her purse, startling her. After fumbling to swipe her passcode, she opened the message from Zach.

Yes or no?

The simple question all but flashed at her, obliterating any chance she had of finding her center any time soon.

She moved her fingers with more self-assurance than the entire rest of her held, defying her indecision, and after a brief hesitation, hit *Send*.

Yes.

chapter six

Zach paced on the sidewalk outside the restaurant. They'd survived day one of DM *checking out operations.* He took a drag off his cigarette and glanced at his watch again. Looking at the time every thirty seconds didn't speed anything up, but he didn't know what else to do. Protocol meant Zach and Scott were obliged to take their guests out for the evening, get to know them off the clock, and play nice.

He didn't want to play nice with the people stealing their company. He dragged his fingers through his hair. Even Selina, the head of HR, hadn't been fun to flirt with. He couldn't get Rae out of his head. An evening breeze brushed his skin, but didn't chase away the heat of frustration.

Car exhaust mixed with the sickly-sweet aroma of the purple and red flowers lining the walkway. The smell wasn't so much relaxing as it was nauseating.

Vance had made passive-aggressive comments from the moment he arrived in the office that morning. Zach closed his eyes and breathed in. The older man encouraged Zach and Scott to bring along their significant others when they went out, a hint of laughter in the suggestion. Zach assumed Vance thought it was amusing based on the whole video-of-Zach's-girlfriend-dumping-him-at-E3-went-viral thing that landed them this situation.

There was no way Vance knew Zach's playboy persona was a façade, but the invitation made it feel like he did. It was a shame Zach couldn't ask Rae.

He cringed. That was a bad train of thought to loiter on. She was the last thing he needed hanging over him right now. The memory of her skin against his. The taste of her kisses. His cock stirred at the reminder of being pressed against her heat, hearing her gasp. The unfinished business in his office with her yesterday.

He was starting to worry Scott wasn't going to show when a familiar SUV pulled up to the valet. The jet-black Escalade was hard to miss, but the G4M3G0D vanity plates were a dead giveaway. A whisper of relief passed over him. An attendant opened the passenger door, and Zach's eyes grew wide as he saw who stepped out. He slid his sunglasses down his nose to make sure he wasn't imagining it.

A white sundress dipped low enough to show a hint of cleavage, but not so low it was inappropriate, had replaced Rae's gauzy top and denim skirt. A sliver of pink peeked out from under one of the shoulder straps. Leave it to her to hide a hint of color under something plain.

The bottom edge of her dress swirled around her legs and ended just above her knees, elongating well-toned legs. The sinking sun caught traces of auburn in her sandy hair, refreshing the lingering memory of strawberry shampoo that had teased Zach since he'd lifted her onto his desk.

Scott had said he was bringing someone and insisted she was just a friend who'd make things more comfortable. Maybe Zach should have asked for more details.

The couple stepped onto the curb, and Zach extended a hand. "Running into you is becoming a habit."

Rae hesitated before accepting the handshake. "No date?" She flushed and ducked her head, leaning into Scott.

Scott wrapped an arm around her waist.

Zach noted the intimate interaction. He had to bite the tip of his tongue to keep from making a joke about the two dating. No reason to make things even more awkward in a situation that already promised to be less than pleasant.

Rae wrapped the strap of her purse around her finger and released it.

Even if Zach knew what to say, their dinner companions heading toward them put a hold on any casual conversation. He pasted on a smile, and taking the hint, Scott turned to face Vance and Selina. Both were dressed in their work clothes still, even though Selina had taken her hair down and let it drape around her shoulders and down her back.

Zach hadn't had a chance to get a good look at her in the office. He took the opportunity now, using his sunglasses to hide his observations. Selina's jacket accentuated every subtle curve on her tall frame without showing any skin between the neck and knees. He let his fantasy trip over what was hidden under the burgundy suit and peach button-down. Black lace, maybe? Or something more practical?

Nothing as fun as hot pink. He glanced at Rae. Maybe she was free after dinner.

"Gentlemen, I'm glad you had time this evening." Vance shook their hands.

Like we had a choice. "It sounded like a great chance to get away and get to know the two of you better."

"I'm sorry to see your girlfriend couldn't join us. Or is she not here yet?" Selina tucked a strand of hair behind her ear.

"I'm afraid work demands so much of my time I don't have a social life." Zach tried not to choke on the pleasantries. He didn't mind the platitudes most of the time, but hated discussing his private life. "There's no girlfriend."

Scott stepped in. "This is Lorraine."

Zach bit back his surprise. Rae was using her full name. Some of the muscles in his neck loosened, and his shoulders relaxed. She was taking this as seriously as they were. Things might go more smoothly with her here.

Vance shook Rae's hand. "We should head inside. I'd hate to keep you out so late you can't finish your homework."

Zach's bit the inside of his cheek. He was seconds away from giving a notably unprofessional response. He knew the older man was rude, but really?

Rae's smile didn't match the way her hand tightened on her purse. "It's all right. I don't usually work at night, but the right people know how to get a hold of me."

"What do you do, dear?" Selina asked.

Rae unzipped the outside pocket on her purse. She plucked two business cards from a small silver case and held them out. "Financial and operations consultant."

Vance tucked the offered card into his jacket pocket. "Interesting. I didn't realize the unemployed got such fancy titles."

Rae's smile twisted but didn't falter. "Neither did I."

"You misunderstand." Zach couldn't keep the edge from his tone. It took most of his remaining restraint to keep from speaking through clenched teeth. "Lorraine is one of the most sought-after names in the country. Anyone worth the C in front of their title is familiar with her name and knows she can make any budget work. A talent like that doesn't tie herself to a single employer."

"That's an impressive recommendation." Selina stepped between Zach and Vance.

Scott cleared his throat. "She deserves it. I think our reservations are waiting?" As they headed toward the restaurant, he wrapped an arm around Rae's waist again and shot Zach a glance, eyebrow raised.

Zach turned away from the unspoken question. He knew better than to let emotion show in business conversations, especially defensiveness. It was going to be a long night. Vance managed to work his way to the front of the group. The doorman greeted them with a nod, holding the smoked glass open.

Zach gave the dimly-lit room a cursory glance. There wasn't a bench seat to be seen in the steakhouse. Burgundy tablecloths and soft candles decorated every table, accessorized by snifters and napkins folded to look like swans. Even though half of the restaurant was full, the quiet chatter barely reached above the clang of silverware on porcelain.

Years ago, when Scott's parents were the ones with the money, and Zach only tagged along when his friend begged, the high-end restaurant would have intimidated him. Since then he'd learned to appreciate the indulgence, especially when there was a good reason to expense the bill.

The conversation shifted to business after they were seated and ordered.

"I was concerned to see your names in the news this weekend." Vance draped his cloth napkin over his knee. "That's not the kind of image we like our executives to project. Reflects poorly on the company as a whole, you understand."

Right, Scott went off at a trade show last week.

Zach wanted to mention DM needed to get used to it. Scott's reputation was built on that kind of bullshit, and the fans ate it up. They'd beat that argument into the ground months ago, though. "Of course. We'll keep that in mind in the future."

Out of the corner of his eye, he saw Rae whisper something to Scott, who forced a smile and nodded back.

Zach tried to ignore his twinge of jealousy, and focused on Selina. She had yet to toss passive-aggressive insults at him. "So how long have you been with the company?"

She chuckled and took a sip of her wine. "Too long."

"You can contact PR if you need any help," Vance said. "I'd hate to see this reflect badly on either of you."

Scott sighed, and Rae whispered something else to him.

"I appreciate the offer. I'll let you know if we can't handle it." Zach forced his smile to stay intact. He desperately needed a smoke.

He almost jumped when a foot traced up his leg. Looking up, he caught Selina's eyes over the top of her glass. She winked before glancing away. Even if he'd been interested, sleeping with the HR rep from his parent company seemed like the fastest way to make things worse. The last thing he needed was to deal with sexual harassment complaints or sensitivity training.

What he needed instead was to walk away for a few minutes and collect his thoughts. He reached for his pocket. "I thought I turned this thing off." He lit up his phone as he pulled it out.

"Something wrong?" Disdain hung heavy in Vance's voice.

Zach stared at the device, feigning concern. "I need to take this. I apologize." He stood, already holding the phone to his ear as he walked away from the table.

He pushed outside, letting the evening air wash over him. Great. Five minutes into dinner, and he was already making weak excuses. He rounded the corner to escape from foot traffic, lit a cigarette, and inhaled deeply. He could make it through the night.

This was what he did. He could ignore the arrogant old man taunting them with what was rightfully theirs.

And he could make plans for after dinner. He took another drag off his smoke and then pecked out a quick message to Rae.

Busy later?

He didn't expect a response during dinner. She was wearing the same cool, professional mask as the rest of them. So he was surprised when his pocket vibrated within a few minutes.

I'm your important call? I'm flattered.

He couldn't help his smile. Like that, a layer of his tension evaporated. *Texting at the table? That'll earn you another jab about your age.*

A few seconds later: *Powdering my nose. Have to get back, and no, I'm not busy later. Want to change that?*

His cock twitched in response to the bold flirting. He inhaled deeply, and then blew smoke through his nose, trying to calm his reaction. His reply was brief. *After dinner?*

Because closure, right?

He smirked, still unable to force his heated blood to cool down. His mind raced ahead with suggestions about the ways they could define closure. Dragging her zipper down. Following it with a trail of kisses along her spine. Drawing his palms up her stomach to cup her breasts…

He sent back, *Of course.*

What happened to sensual seduction? she asked

That's what this is. He knew better, but this *was*

fun. Light-hearted and simple, the way the two of them should be. He wasn't sure where the thought came from, but as it rolled around in his head, it felt right.

God, you're an ass.

He laughed at his phone and the empty air. More of his tension evaporated from his tight muscles. She might have meant the comment cruelly, but something told him she was having as much fun as him. *Only because I can't stop thinking about how incredible yours is.*

My ass?

And the rest of you.

**Blush* Don't be late.*

A half smile stayed with him while he finished his smoke. He hovered outside for a few more minutes to let the smell dissipate and then headed back to dinner. Rae had already rejoined the group and was swapping stories with Selina about whether it was better to give someone a written warning right off or talk to them first. When Selina took the hard, fast line of no exceptions, Zach was even more relieved he'd ignored her flirting. Not that she held a candle to Rae.

"Everything all right?" Scott asked as soon as Zach was seated.

Shit, Zach hadn't come up with an excuse. This entire thing was screwing with his head. His brain kicked an answer to his mouth without pausing to let him process. "Broker."

Scott scowled. "Of course."

Vance laughed. "At least you're planning for your future."

Rae gave Zach a brief glance. She looked away before he could be sure if what he saw dancing in her brown eyes was laughter.

He resisted the urge to call off the night early. Knowing what was waiting for him would at least make things more tolerable.

chapter seven

Rae perched on the edge of Chloe's couch, intertwining her fingers and then unwinding them again. Should she change? She'd already stowed her shoes in the guest room. She smoothed the sundress over her knees, even though there was no one around to be modest for. Her sister was spending the night with Jordan, so Rae had the place to herself. Was she making a mistake with Zach?

No. She kept thinking she might feel differently each time she asked the question, but she couldn't convince herself this was a bad idea.

She jumped at a knock on the door, hand flying to her hammering heart, and giggled at her own reaction. *Remember to breathe.* She tried to take her time crossing the room to answer.

"Hey." It was the only thing she could manage when she saw Zach. She stepped aside, using the excuse to study him when he entered. The tailored jacket hung off his shoulders perfectly, and the slacks made his ass look fantastic. She liked the view when he was around.

Her hostess instinct kicked in when she couldn't think of anything else to say. She latched the door and leaned back against it. "Can I get you anything?"

"You."

That was corny. And she didn't care. Her lips and skin still tingled with the memories from his office, and that was only a kiss. She forced down her hesitation and stepped closer. "Easy enough."

"Easy's not the word I would have used." He rested a hand on her cheek and kissed her softly. His mouth trailed down her jaw to her throat and over her shoulder. "I could go for intoxicating. Or distracting."

He was good at that. Her body yielded even as her mind tried to stay in control. Getting rid of the sexual tension between them was definitely a good idea. She tilted her head back, sinking into every new sensation. "It's not a negotiation."

"Hmm…" The sound rumbled through her skin. "Says you." He slipped a finger under the shoulder strap of her dress and slid it down to the top of her breast before moving back up again. "Pink bra." He kissed along her collarbone. "Flared skirt." His hand rested on her waist. "Wait. What were we talking about?"

She relaxed further. This wasn't the salesman who worked his verbal bullshit magic at dinner or the guy who didn't hesitate to ask for a waitress's phone number. Would he actually let down his defenses for the night and let her see the real him? She was trying to deny it, but she missed that person—the banter, the fun, the long hours just talking.

She couldn't separate the past from now, regardless of how hard she tried? Was this a mistake?

The desire flooding her said *no*. The ache of the past disagreed.

"You're too quiet." He nipped her neck, and she gasped. "That's a start. Something on your mind?"

No way was she spoiling the moment by voicing her doubts or observations. She broke away with a smile, pushed his jacket off his shoulders, and hung it on a hook by the door. "Only one thing."

He grasped her fingers with one hand, pulling her close while wrapping his other arm around her waist. He kissed her lightly again. "The kind of thing you'd be willing to describe in vivid…" He caught her bottom lip between his teeth "…lurid…" He bit her earlobe, voice barely a whisper "…detail?

Every new sensation sent another spark through her, making her lightheaded. She pressed against him, memorizing the way her body molded to his. "I'm not the wordsmith you are, and what I had in mind is a lot more hands on."

He slid around until he was standing behind her. His lips traced up the back of her neck, breath hot against her skin. "I like the way you think."

She tilted her head back and rested it against his chest. He glided his palms up her stomach, the light but confident touch sending tingles of desire through her. This was simple, how was it so enthralling? She didn't care, as long as he kept going.

His nose tickled her shoulder then her ear. "Strawberry, right?" His question was soft. "Basic, but seductive."

"I'll keep that in mind." Every sensation was something new to lose herself in, and she wasn't sure which to give her attention to next.

He brushed the bottom of her breast. Temperature rising, she gasped and pressed closer to his body. Wetness grew between her legs at the feeling of his hard cock against her butt. He was as turned on as she was—the realization amped her desire another notch.

He squeezed gently until he reached her nipple. He pinched the hard nub through her dress, increasing the pressure as her moans grew louder.

She grasped a fistful of skirt when she couldn't find anything else to hold onto. He glided his free hand down her bare arm, covered her fist, and then continued lower. He inched the fabric up until his fingers reached the outside of her thigh.

"You have no idea…" He pulled her skirt higher, nails raking lightly up her skin. "…how hard it was to concentrate at dinner, knowing you were waiting for me."

It took focus to form words, but she managed to find her voice. "I have a little bit of an idea."

Still sliding her dress up, he reached her waist. The air caressed her now-exposed leg, and she shivered at the contrast with his hot touch. He squeezed her tit. The hint of pain mingled with pleasure, and tore a moan from her throat. Letting go of the edge of her dress, he sought out her mound with his fingers, and rubbed through her panties. She shifted her weight to bring herself closer to his hand.

He kissed along the back of her neck. "Is this what you want?" He shoved the thin, cotton crotch aside. His groan mingled with her gasp when he touched her slit. "God, you wax? I love these surprises."

She didn't have a reply. All her attention was on his hands, and her breathing grew shallow.

His fingers dipped between her folds. "And you're so wet."

Her back arched when he found her clit.

"There?" He placed a finger on either side of the swollen button.

She nodded. Speaking was beyond her grasp right now. He worked his hands in rhythm tweaking her nipple and stroking her sex. She wrapped a hand around his left arm, nails digging in. His pace stayed steady, almost maddeningly so. Enough to build a solid rush inside, but not grant her release.

She bit the inside of her cheek, torn between covering his hand with hers to pick up the rhythm and seeing how much longer she could sink into the delicious sensation. She hovered on the edge of climax, and her mind fuzzed.

"You're so intoxicating." His hot breath teased her skin. He kissed along her neck again, harder than before, nipping and then sucking the tender flesh. The sharp new sting rolled through her, and her hips bucked in response. He increased his speed on her clit, rubbing harder at the same time.

The various points of contact—pleasure, pain, teasing, kissing, prompting—tore an orgasm from her and stole her breath. She was only vaguely aware of her cries as she came. She rocked in time with him, pulling away when the touch became too much. He slowed his attentions and eased off, but didn't let go of her.

Her legs wobbled, and his hands moved to her stomach to hold her upright while drawing her against his chest. She struggled to find her breath.

He kissed along the edge of her ear, voice low. "I want you unable to stand when I'm done." He slid his fingers up her arms, raising goose bumps and then pointed her toward the doors at the far end of the living room. "Right or left bedroom?"

"Left." She was surprised she managed even the simple word. How had he done that to her?

He nudged her forward and then into the guest bedroom. They stopped just short of the bed, and he whirled them both, so she faced him, her back to the bed. She reached up to loosen his tie then pulled it over his head, keeping her head tilted back enough to look him in the eye.

"Not so fast. What if we need that?" He grabbed her wrist, and a new shock of want flooded her.

"For…?" She trailed off as his meaning sank in, and a heat filled her cheeks. Surrendering that kind of control to him opened up an entirely new wave of doubt mixed with desire. "Oh."

He took it from her and set it on the nightstand. "Maybe not tonight." He winked.

The teasing was enough to make her fumble when she started at the top of his shirt to undo his buttons, but she managed to unfasten them without too much trouble. Seconds later, he stood shirtless in front of her.

He looked good. How did someone who spent all their time in an office and on the road have that kind of wiry definition in their chest? She traced her fingers along the muscle, memorizing each line.

He inhaled sharply, tangled his fingers with hers, and moved his other hand to her back, holding her tight.

She kissed along his collarbone, down his chest, and then flicked her tongue over his nipple. Desire spun in her thoughts when he growled. He caressed her shoulder blade above the line of her dress, and then she felt the fabric pull away when he slid the zipper down.

He dragged the straps off her shoulders, and the dress pooled around her feet on the floor. She kicked it aside. Warmth mingled with self-consciousness when he held her at arm's length, his gaze devouring her as she stood in front of him in nothing but a hot-pink bra and white, high-cut bikini briefs.

"Definitely enjoying the view." His voice was low and heavy. He dipped his head and glided his mouth along her collarbone.

She sank back into the moment. Her hands moved lower. His breathing changed when she found his belt. She managed to undo the buckle and then his slacks without tying her fingers in knots.

Please let my hands stay steady. The tremor of enjoyment thrumming through her made it difficult, but she'd figure it out somehow.

Boxers. That was sexy. She brushed his cock through the thin fabric, and he groaned. He was big, she realized as she stroked him teasingly. Her imagination skipped forward a few steps to what it would feel like to be stretched by him.

She dipped her hand inside his underwear, searching out his bare skin. When she wrapped her fingers around his shaft, he bit hard on her shoulder. At least she wasn't the only one lost in the moment. The thought increased her arousal another notch.

"This is killing me." His voice was rough. Almost jagged. "I know I promised seduction, but God damn it, you're irresistible. I need to bury myself inside you. Fuck you hard, until neither of us can think."

The hunger in his words stole her reason, and lit up her senses. Still stroking him, she kissed him again. He hissed and reached for her when she let go, but she stepped out of reach. He could have some control, but she wasn't surrendering it all.

His smile returned when she unhooked her bra and let it fall to the floor. She pushed her panties off next and scooted onto the bed to sit with her back straight, legs tucked to the side, and chest thrust out. The pose felt a little ridiculous, but the way his heated attention traveled up and down her form erased her doubt.

He dropped his boxers and bent for a moment, fiddling with his discarded slacks. *What the—? Oh, condom.* She flushed. At least one of them still had a grasp on reason.

Seconds later, he had wrapped himself up. He crawled onto the bed next to her, nudged her onto her back, and kissed her deeply. He cupped her breast as their tongues danced together.

He slid his hand down her arm, and then rolled onto his back, tugging. "I want you on top." He stroked the inside of her thigh. "I want to watch you riding me."

The order heated her thoughts. She straddled him and slid down his hips until his cock hovered at her opening. She lowered herself enough to tease, but not to let him penetrate.

He grasped her hips, digging his fingers into her pelvis, and thrust his hips up. When he pushed deep inside her, she cried out. So much for drawing out the moment. Her swimming head didn't care. Each time his flesh met hers, a new tremor of pleasure spiked through her.

They found a fast, frantic rhythm, and every time she slid down, he hit something deep inside. His breathing came in short grunts, and his gaze never left her. He slid his hands to her thighs, thumbs stroking the flesh before moving higher. "Play with your tits for me."

The request, combined with the thought of performing, dragged her closer to the edge. She grabbed the soft flesh, kneading, and rolling her nipples between her fingers. His breathing was shallow. He had to be close. She was. The familiar scents of the guest room—fabric softener and furniture polish—mingled with sex and his sharp, clean smell. Every time he grunted or groaned, her chest clenched and her need swelled.

She gasped when he found her clit with his thumb. Each time she bounced, he bumped the swollen button. It should have been too tender for the harsh attention, but he pressed against her, drawing a new level of pleasure form her. For the second time that night, orgasm shredded through her. She lost herself in the moment, pounding against him, pussy clenching around his cock.

His grunts ran together, and he tightened his hand around her thigh. He arched his back with a final groan. His pace slowed until he sank back against the comforter with a sigh.

A euphoric exhaustion permeated her, and she bent at the waist to rest her cheek against his chest. She didn't know how long they lay like that, trying to catch their breath. He trailed his fingers through her hair, not saying anything. This shouldn't feel so comfortable. Screw what it should or shouldn't be. It felt as right as everything leading up to it.

After several minutes, she rolled off him and rested her head on his shoulder instead. She didn't want to ask the question knocking in the back of her head. An irrational concern told her if she didn't ask, he couldn't give the wrong response. She forced the words out, voice soft. "Do you have to get home?"

"Mmm..." He grabbed a tissue off the nightstand. After stripping off the condom, he wrapped it up, the tossed it in the trashcan nearby.

The vague answer dug deeper than she thought possible. Was he brushing her off? It shouldn't matter, but she couldn't ignore the hope he was sticking around. She tried to keep her tone light. "That's not an answer."

He trailed his fingers up her spine, drawing her closer with the light touch. "Something wore me out." The energy was gone from his voice, but the playfulness was still there. "I don't know if I should drive."

Relief flitted through her. This was a dangerous line to walk, but if it was only for one night, she was grabbing as many pleasant memories as possible. She smiled against his shoulder and kissed along the bare skin. "You'd probably better stay here, then. Just to be safe."

She shouldn't be taking it so far. This was a

mistake, but the warm body next to her, the strong arm around her, told her regret could wait until tomorrow.

♥ ♥ ♥

Rae rolled onto her back, still wrapped in sleep. Something didn't feel right. The thought jolted her toward consciousness. What was wrong?

She reached her arms out to either side. Nothing. Well, blanket, twisted sheets, and a pillow she didn't usually keep there, but no one else.

She sighed and closed her eyes again. Of course Zach was already gone. What did she expect? It wasn't as if they were going to have coffee and breakfast together and chat the day away.

At least he saved her the trouble of an awkward goodbye. She sat up, hair falling around her face as she slouched forward. They'd rewritten their ending, just like he suggested. They could be in the same room together again, and she'd be done with the childish swooning. Starting over, as friends and nothing more, would be easier now without animosity haunting them.

It was closure. It had been incredible, but that chapter of her past was finished.

Her phone buzzed on the nightstand, and she grabbed it out of habit. She couldn't hide her smile as she flipped through Zach's messages.

Had an early meeting, or I would have said goodbye.

Best closure ever.

Enjoy your day.

She climbed out of bed. Why did that make her

feel better? Nothing else had changed, but knowing she wasn't the only one it had left an impression on helped. Now she just had to focus on reminding herself an impression was all she needed.

Shower, then start digging up her next contract. Last night wasn't enough to make her forget *they* ended a long time ago. Throwing herself into her job hunt should get rid of the lingering traces of something she couldn't name.

chapter eight

Zach tried to ignore the one-on-one meetings going on in the conference room. Vance was interviewing everyone individually to *get to know his new people better.* Zach didn't like the sound of it, but hadn't been able to craft a valid objection.

He made himself comfortable in the chair across from Scott's desk and waited for acknowledgment. Back in the day, when they were decorating, he'd given Scott crap for the plastic mesh on metal legs. Even though the seats *kind of* matched the modern décor everywhere else, they were butt-ugly. Zach realized over time they were also the most comfortable chairs in the office.

Magazine reviews and industry awards glared at him; black frames against white walls reminded him how much they had poured into the company.

Scott glanced in his direction but didn't pull his attention away from the three flat screens between them. "You score?"

Zach studied him. Had Rae already said something? No. The question was too vague. "Huh?"

Scott nodded toward the conference rooms. "Miss   Bun-so-tight-it-has-to-give-her-a-migraine, who was winking at you through the entire evening? I'll take that as a no."

Zach shrugged. That should be his segue. The entire reason he was here. This wasn't the kind of secret he could keep, and it wasn't as if it was a big deal he'd slept with Rae. They both agreed it was an outlet. A means to an end. So why was he hesitating?

Scott typed a few more things, still not pulling his attention from his work. "Probably smart. Odds are she fucks like a woman who knows she's attractive."

The statement sent a rush of images through Zach's head made his cock perk to life: Rae's unique combination of bold seduction and hesitation, the way she slid against him, her soft curves yielding to his attentions. He shifted in his seat, trying to be subtle about adjusting himself. "I assume." He didn't want to be talking about Selina. Someone else was on his mind. "Speaking of last night, you could have said something."

Scott studied him for a moment, eyes hard, before turning back to his computer. "You didn't call that yourself? Besides, you didn't go home with her, what do you care?"

Scott had to know Zach was talking about his bringing Rae to dinner with no warning, not about Selina. Zach pinched the bridge of his nose. His entire week was going to be filled with political games; he didn't want to play them with Scott. "Not about that."

Scott shook his head, clicking on something, generating a series of beeps. "I told you I was bringing a friend."

He needed a fix. Stupid indoor anti-smoking laws. Zach sighed. "Really? And it slipped your mind to mention your *friend* was..." He trailed off, mentally restructuring his sentence so it sounded less emotional. "Her?"

"You could have asked for a name. Are the two of you on speaking terms or not? Because really, a decade of listening to you not talk about each other has worn on me."

"I wouldn't have guessed." Zach couldn't keep the sarcasm from his voice.

"So no issues, then." Scott's tone shifted to something less casual, and his attention was fully on the conversation now. "You can be in the same room together, and no one has to plan around your childish spat."

Why was there so much aggravation there? Zach rolled the words over in his head, examining the delivery as much as the meaning. Was that a hint of possession in Scott's voice? "No issues."

Scott shook his head. "Glad to hear something that happened in high school hasn't left you permanently scarred."

That was definitely a sneer in his words. Zach needed to watch his step on this one, though he still wasn't sure why. He forced his smile to look casual and kept a teasing tone in his voice. "Like you're one to talk."

Scott glared at Zach. "You know I'm not stupid, right?"

That had come out of nowhere. "I wonder sometimes, but for the most part, yes."

"You go out of your way to avoid each other for

the majority of a decade." Scott spoke through clenched teeth. "The only girl besides Kelly to ever dump you. Suddenly she's giving you googly eyes at breakfast, she's in your office with the door locked, and she's texting you in the middle of a fucking business dinner."

Zach couldn't hide his surprise. So that hadn't gone unnoticed after all, and still he couldn't bring himself to own up to it. "I was talking to—"

"Your broker. Yeah, I get it. That short little guy who lives at the end of the rainbow. Because, really? You've got a broker?"

"Your point?"

"She's not a game. This isn't the woman you tag at a trade show because you're bored."

That settled it. Zach wasn't mentioning last night at all. Since it had only been a one-time deal, there was no reason. "I get that. You can pretend she's your little sister all you want. I don't have any plans to go after her."

Not again. Even if he was still thinking about the night before. He certainly wasn't wondering what would have happened if he'd been able to stick around that morning. Talk, learn more about what she'd been up to in her own words, find out what other buttons she had that made her moan. That was what memories were for.

"Whatever." Scott shook his head. "I don't want to do this with you."

That made two of them. Maybe a change of subject was the best idea. "At least she's not the HR director, right?"

"Good call. You get any good intel?"

Zach felt the tension leak away and gladly slid into the new topic. "Jordan says he's quitting if they start making the rules. Chloe says they'd better give her a pay raise if she has to put up with their bullshit. Marketing is drooling over DM's media budget."

Scott chuckled. "So, typical day at the office?"

"Pretty much." Zach made a mental note to change the topic if Rae came up again. Nothing new there, except his reasons. "I talked to Jim this morning."

Jim was the attorney reviewing their buy-out offers.

Scott's posture shifted. His hands fell away from the keyboard, and he sat straight up. "And?"

"They've finished looking everything over. Not really any surprises, just a couple of things they want clarified before we sign." Zach knew that wasn't the news Scott wanted, but it was all he had.

Scott folded his arms on his desk and dropped his head into them. The desk muffled his response. "What if I don't want to be bought out?"

Like talking to a five-year-old. Zach cringed inwardly at the thought. This was hard on both of them. "Still waiting on that other option we don't have?"

"For as long as I can."

Zach should argue. This was getting out of hand, and they didn't have a lot of time left to make their decision. He didn't want to give this up any more than Scott did, though.

They talked a few minutes longer, then Scott headed back to his office.

Zach was still stuck in the loop of the

conversation. Frustrated with Scott's refusal to accept reality. Irritated with himself for glossing over Rae.

Thinking about Rae.

The one place he shouldn't be focused. *Closure.* Was that what they had?

Nothing was resolved.

That wasn't completely true. The resentment was gone, which left plenty of room for the daydreams and fresh memories to assault him. So was it worth it?

It was fucking worth it. He'd do it again in a heartbeat. He still needed to move on, both from Rae and this company.

It shouldn't be so difficult to leave the past behind. Maybe he needed to lose himself in noise so loud he couldn't think, and a couple of overpriced drinks.

Drinking on a Tuesday night seemed like a bad idea, but those were working for him recently.

Rae tried to make out the click of her swizzle stick against her glass amid the chatter in the bar. She stared at the milky brown drink swirling around ice. What was she doing there?

Someone slid into the seat next to her. The smell of cologne mixed with the alcohol on his breath was so strong she almost gagged. He loosened his tie and undid the top button on his shirt.

Rae tried to decide if he was cute. It was hard to tell. He didn't stand out from any other twenty-somethings in the bar—he was trying too hard to prove he was someone.

He looked in her direction, and she turned her attention to her drink.

He leaned closer, his breathy question making her eyes water. "Hey, beautiful. Is it true chubby girls try harder in bed?"

She fiddled with the edge of her shirt and moved to a different stool, not bothering to answer. It had taken a long time to get over the image issues she'd had as a teenager. Several of which stemmed from the fact Zach had only dated thin girls before her. She wasn't overweight—but she'd never had the narrow waist and slim figure that would lead anyone to mistake her for a supermodel. That didn't mean comments about her lack of Photoshop physique hurt any less.

A series of basketball games blared in the background, overlapping each other and clashing with the chatter. A voice whispered in the back of her head that if she wanted to take her mind off Zach, a sports bar filled with young businessmen just like him, but slimier, probably wasn't the way to do it.

She had the same thought two hours earlier, but had hoped the alcohol would make it better. Now she was just drunk enough to realize she wasn't in the mood for a cheap stand-in.

"What's your poison, hot stuff?" The stranger's alcohol-laden breath landed on her cheek, and he wrapped an arm around her waist.

A chill crawled under her skin. She jerked away from the grabby douche. "Nothing you can afford."

"Like you're going to find a better offer."

A hand rested at the small of her back. "She said

she's not interested." Zach's familiar voice erased the cold roaring through her.

Her heart stuttered to a stall and then sped up tenfold. What was he doing there? And what would it take to keep his hand there a little longer?

Drunk Douche appraised Zach. "Not in you."

"Maybe not." Zach's arm brushed her spine. "But at least I can take *no* for an answer."

Rae watched the scene unfold, horror tingeing her fascination. Her skull winced in protest, or maybe it was the three white Russians reminding her she hadn't eaten that night.

"Slut." Drunk Douche stumbled into the barstool in his haste to get away.

It was tempting to let Zach go after Drunk Douche, but Rae forced herself to put a restraining hand on his arm. She wasn't some princess who needed a knight in shining armor, but knowing that didn't stop the unexpected rescue from warming her. "He's not worth it."

When he whirled back to face her, his snarl morphed into a soft smile. He dropped into the stool next to her. "At least let me pick up your tab."

He was being sweet. What did he want? She hated the thought. She also wanted his hand on her back again. Wanted to lean against his shoulder and forget putting him behind her was part of the reason she'd been drinking.

She shook her head but stopped when the room tilted at strange angles. "Already covered, but thank you."

He moved her drink away from her. "You look wobbly."

"Only a little." She needed him closer again, so she could lean on him. No, she didn't. She was fine. "Maybe it's time to call it a night."

She hopped off the stool. Her heel hooked on a rung, and she stumbled, destroying her attempt at a cool getaway.

Zach caught her, one hand on her shoulder, and the other on her hip to help her stand again.

A whisper of his aftershave washed over her, and she swallowed. Damn it, she didn't need him there. A taunting voice in the back of her mind pointed out he was probably here to pick up a girl. Though her intent was similar, the realization drove home how one-time last night had been. She hurried to right herself, and almost fell backward again in the process.

He studied her for a minute, concern heavy in his eyes. "You're calling a cab, right?"

"No." She wasn't that drunk. "I need my car… Because reasons." Which really, she didn't. The rental could stay in the lot until tomorrow, and she wouldn't miss it. Stubbornness kept her from admitting it.

When she wobbled again he grabbed her car keys and wrapped an arm around her waist. "Can I give you a ride home, m'lady?"

That felt good. Her entire body tilted toward the contact. She frowned and straightened. How had she been jostled into this? "I'm fine, thanks." She reached for her keys but lost her footing when he yanked them out of reach.

"Yeah, you're not. You don't have to leave with me, but you're not driving."

She wanted to protest again, but being so close to him made it hard to think. She put some space between them. "Fine. Whatever." She winced at his raised eyebrows and pursed lips. "A ride home would be nice."

They made their way to the parking lot. He steered her toward one of the flashier cars in the lot—a Porsche Cayman. How many of the guys inside could have paid cash for a vehicle like this? He unlocked her door and held her arm until she was seated. The interior filled her head with his scent and leather, and made her thoughts dance faster.

It didn't escape her when he took the opportunity to watch her skirt ride up. Good. At least she wasn't the only one this was affecting. She took her time smoothing the hem out again.

An awkward silence descended between them as he pulled onto the road. A string of questions spilled through her head, some ice-breakers, others flirty, and others filled with self-righteous indignation. She couldn't focus enough to figure out which direction she wanted to go. Her mouth made the decision without her brain's permission. "So is the ride home a clever excuse to try and get me in bed again?"

His eyes narrowed. "This is the one and only time I'll ever say this. Never, not before, not now, not in the future, will we do anything while you're under the influence."

What was wrong with her? He'd rescued her—not just from Drunk Douche, or having to take a cab home, but from an evening she didn't want after all—and she was insulting him in return.

He sighed and fished a pack of smokes from his shirt pocket. He stuck one to his lips then obviously thought better of it.

"You can smoke; I don't care."

"You sure?"

"It's your car. Besides, you're doing me a favor."

"Am I the only one struggling with this?" He rolled the window down before lighting up.

Rae stared at him, surprised by the question and the frustration behind it. She couldn't lie. Not about this, and not to him. "No."

"I've thought about this a lot more than I should since you came back." He exhaled, smoke drifting out the window and vanishing in to the night. "We're in the past. What we were doesn't matter. So why do I keep coming back to you being here now?"

Figured. She was struggling to force the alcohol aside enough to hold up her half the conversation, and he was digging into her head and tugging on the one thread she wanted to ignore. "I don't have an answer."

Zach hadn't only been in the bar a few minutes when he caught sight of a familiar blonde. Irrational jealousy surged inside when he saw another guy sitting next to Rae, and it turned to fury when Zach watched her try to shrug the guy off.

Now he was spilling his guts, and he didn't want to be.

But she was listening, she sounded as stalled as he was, and he needed to get the thoughts out of his head.

"I know I promised rewriting our ending would give me closure, but I can't seem to let our breakup go, regardless of how long ago it happened, or how many misunderstandings we cleared up." Frustration surged inside. He pulled the elastic from his ponytail and raked his fingers through his hair. "It's not because you dumped me, or left town without even saying goodbye, or told everyone I was the one pushing you into a future you didn't want. None of that would have mattered if you had been anyone else."

Her silence was impossible to interpret. Did she feel any of this the way he did?

There was an ache behind his ribs that wouldn't go away. He needed answers. He needed to empty his head. He needed...

Not her. Finishing that thought led down a bad road. So he grabbed more words instead. "I trusted you. More than anyone. You were my confidant and my equal. You were the only person I could be myself around. Even with Scott there were certain behaviors I kept in check because of his parents."

He'd hated that. Always having to be on his best behavior. It was second nature now, but sometimes he just wanted to say *fuck it* and not live by other people's rules. He'd though he had that with Rae. "I thought we could talk about anything, and when you walked out, I realized the only conversation that mattered was the one thing you kept to yourself."

He flicked his cigarette out the window and exhaled, breath shaky. "You made assumptions. I saw it happening and hoped it would solve itself. We thought we were sharing ourselves with each other, and instead it was this verbal dance, both of us too stubborn to yield. And it still is."

"You're right." Her voice was tiny.

He gave a short laugh. Shouldn't that admission make him feel better? What was wrong with him? Did he think they could go back? That wouldn't happen. He was fooling himself to believe otherwise. "We're kind of fucked up like that, I guess."

"I'm sorry."

He pulled his car into her spot in visitor parking, and turned to her. Exhaustion and regret mingled with heavy sadness. "Me too."

<h1 style="text-align:center">chapter nine</h1>

Rae tossed her controller on the coffee table and flung her hands in the air. "Owned!"

The final score blinked back from the large screen TV, taunting and backing up her exclamation. She'd beaten Scott at a video game. She couldn't believe it. Sure, it was *Tetris*, but still. It was the principle.

"Not," Scott said.

"Yuh-huh." She giggled. This was so much better than letting her mind replay the conversation with Zach. Like it had for the last three days. She didn't have a solution, but his tone, his words, the fact that she agreed, all gnawed at her. Everything he said echoed how she felt, and she didn't know what to do about it. Ignoring it wasn't working. Hanging out with Scott was a temporary reprieve, because it let her pretend she could still cling to part of that past. "Guess I'm not a noob after all, noob."

"Oh yeah?" Scott lunged forward and tickled her.

"Ack!" Her giggles squealed through the condo. She fell back on the couch, leather creaking beneath her as she tried to get away. Her shirt slid up her stomach, exposing more of her flesh the more she resisted. His palms were warm against her skin. The more she squirmed under him, the more her body reacted. She paused, aware of how close he was.

He's good looking. But he's not Zach.

Rae didn't want him to be. She wanted both of them in her life, in different ways.

She rested a palm on Scott's chest. "This isn't us."

"It could be." He searched her face.

It really couldn't be. Even if she wasn't hung up on Zach. *Hung up?* Yeah. "It really couldn't. I'd do anything for you."

"But I won't do that." Scott sang in a cheesy Meatloaf imitation. He sighed, straightened up, and helped pull her into a sitting position.

I'm sorry. That wasn't the right thing to say. She wasn't. Why was this all coming together and falling apart right now?

Because I've avoided it for so long.

She couldn't anymore. What was happening?

A loud pounding interrupted them. Both of them froze, Scott's gaze locked on hers.

She ignored the whisper of relief trickling through her. If she had to split her angst between defining her relationship with Scott, and figuring out what the fuck was going on with Zach, her brain was going to collapse. "You should probably get that."

The doorbell rang, followed by another round of pounding. He stood. "Yeah. I guess so."

What kind of random visitors did he get on a Saturday afternoon? As soon as the question crossed her mind, she had awkward flashes of the Friday she'd gotten into town, and watching him served with the letter that might as well have been a death sentence.

Her gut flipped when she saw a FedEx guy in the doorway.

"Letter for Scott McAllister. Can you sign?"

Scott reached for the digital clipboard. "Sure."

The man in purple studied the signature for a second. "Last name?"

"McAllister?"

"Great. Thanks." He handed over the envelope and was gone.

Scott's frown deepened when he looked at her.

She smiled, but the expression faded again quickly. It was just a coincidence, right? A random delivery that had nothing to do with bad news? The DM logo glared at her from across the room. "I'm starting to think you shouldn't take any more overnight letter deliveries."

He raised an eyebrow and then shook his head. He flopped down on the couch next to her and dropped the envelope into his lap. The soft overhead lights glared off the stark white card stock.

The silence sank in, a heavy buzz growing in Rae's ears. Finally, she nudged his arm with her shoulder. "You have to open it sometime. It's just a letter."

He nodded but still didn't move.

She didn't blame him. Even her gut churned at the idea of what might be in there, and she wasn't one of them. After the week of downs they'd had, she wouldn't want to see what the parent company said either. She took the letter from his lap and yanked the pull strip. The tearing sound echoed in the emptiness. She dropped the contents into her hand, and the embossed letterhead glinted in the light.

It took willpower not to read it herself, but this wasn't for her. She handed the short stack of papers back to Scott, then tucked her hands into her lap.

He muttered as he read and had his phone out within minutes.

She rose. "I should go."

He tugged her wrist, and she dropped back onto the couch. "This won't take long. Hey," he said into the phone. "You get this?"

She hovered at the edge of the cushion, not having to ask who he was talking to. *So awkward.*

Scott set the phone on the coffee table. "At least they're still paying us." His joke sounded forced. "I mean, the suspension is only temporary, right?"

"For now." Zach's voice echoed from the speakerphone. "You haven't shown the layoff list to anyone, have you?"

Rae's back went rigid. Now was definitely her cue to leave.

Scott shook his head, brow furrowed. "Just a sec," he whispered to her. In a normal volume he said, "I just got it. Who would I show?" He stood and paced while he talked, socks shuffling against plush carpet.

"I don't know. Anyone else who might have a personal stock in that list. Or someone who knows the people on it."

The sick feeling grew in Rae's stomach. Part of it was attached to Zach's response; he was talking about her. But the rest of it hadn't found a reason yet.

"I don't have to show you," Scott said to the phone. "You already know." He gave Rae a weak smile and a wink.

"Clever. Just, maybe this once, keep it between us?" There was a surrender in the plea that surprised

Rae.

"I'm not stupid." Scott wouldn't look at her.

And her ill feeling grew. A layoff list they wouldn't tell her about. *Chloe.*

"We need a plan," Scott said.

Zach made a noise that landed somewhere between a growl and a hiss. "We have a plan. Cash out, walk away. There's a decent severance offer for them, and they're all talented people."

"That's not a plan. It's retreat." Scott's hands clenched into fists.

"Semantics." Zach spat the word. "Call it cut-and-run, if you want. It's our only option."

Rae's thoughts tilted and dipped, weighted with concern for her sister. She only half registered the volatile conversation. At least Rae could be here in person for Chloe.

"We can't fix it." Zach sounded exhausted. "What are the you missing about the term *hostile takeover*? It's not our company anymore."

Scott flopped back against the couch cushions. There was a resignation in his voice that had never been there before. "Yeah, same old shit. We'll do what we have to Monday."

"You're sure?" Zach asked.

Rae frowned, hating the surrender. She should stop by the grocery store on the way back to Chloe's. Stock up on ice cream. Plan on her sister crashing hard when she heard the news. When would she find out? Not before Monday, so at least she could enjoy her weekend.

"Later." Scott leaned forward and disconnected the phone. He dropped his head into his hands. "This sucks."

Rae didn't know what to do besides agree.

Rae had no idea where she was going. Not home. Her afternoon with Scott tanked hardcore. She wasn't in the mood to sit in Chloe's apartment and stare blankly at the TV. Besides, she needed to collect herself before she saw her sister again. This wasn't her news to deliver, and Rae wasn't sure she could keep it to herself in her current frame of mind.

She navigated her car mindlessly through the streets. Her already scattered thoughts fragmented further when she realized she'd landed less than a block from Zach's house. She wouldn't know where he lived, but Chloe had pointed it out once as they drove through the affluent neighborhood on the side of the mountain.

What was she doing here? *It's not as though a face-to-face conversation will change things.* So why wasn't she turning around and heading in the opposite direction?

There had to be something they'd missed. Scott wasn't any help on that front. He wanted to fix things but had no ideas. Maybe it was time to approach it from a different angle. She had no idea what she was going to say to Zach, but she knocked anyway.

The door swung open, and he stood on the other side. His body was rigid, his words clipped. "I'm just going to assume, given the convenient timing, that you know about the layoffs. Did he call you the minute he hung up with me?"

"I was already at his place."

He rolled his eyes and stepped aside. "So much for keeping things quiet. Fair warning. I love Scott dearly, but I can't deal with the denial anymore. Cord is over. And if you're here to reinforce his delusions, so is this conversation."

She stepped into the foyer, hands jammed into her shorts pockets. "Why do you do that?"

"Do…?" He looked her over, gaze lingering on its way to her face.

A thrilled chill ran through her at the scrutiny. "Try so hard to dominate the conversation." She grimaced as the unfortunate choice of words sank in.

The corner of his mouth twitched. "Is that really the phrasing you want to go with?"

She sighed and shook her head. This wasn't the worst time to be assaulted by memories of riding him, feeling him plunge deep inside her, hearing his grunts… "That's not why I'm here."

"Right. The why. I'm still not clear on that."

She didn't know either. She grasped for any answer at all, in the midst of her frustration. "If this is going to devastate Chloe, how is it not devouring you?"

"Do you really believe that?" He turned away, and strode into the living room.

She followed. "You're not really convincing me—or anyone else—otherwise."

He stopped behind the sofa, leaned against it, and then faced her again. "Because letting it show doesn't do anyone any good." He raked his fingers through his hair. He snagged the ponytail holder, yanked it out with a snarl, and tossed it aside. "We don't own the company anymore. We're not even being offered noticeable shares of DM as part of our buyout. We're not in charge. It's all gone. I'm not surrendering because I want to, or because I like watching people I trust and respect suffer. We don't have a choice." Each word was clipped and distinct.

The hint of vulnerability dug deep. Seeing this side of him gnawed at her. Made her want to tug at the loose thread and see what else she could reveal. She crossed her arms and rested her butt against the back of the couch, her hip brushing his. "It just seems so final. It doesn't even directly impact me, and still it hurts to see it all ripped away."

He dragged in a long breath. "How do you think I feel? I don't know what else to tell you. I don't have a magic answer. We can't talk or buy our way out of this. Scott's genius won't save us. I can't spin some bullshit for the internet to make us shine. Do you think I want it this way?"

"No." An empty pit grew in her chest, aching for him. For Chloe and Scott. "I'm sorry."

"It's a pretty common sentiment these days." He shifted his weight, and his arm pressed against hers.

A shock of warmth rushed through her at the contact. It was comfortable. A distraction from the looming bad news. Sleeping together hadn't granted them closure. Giving into the attraction again wouldn't yield a different result. "I shouldn't have bothered you. I'll let you get back to… Whatever"

"For what it's worth…" He grabbed her arm loosely and tugged, prompting her to face him. He pulled her between his legs, dropped his hands to her hips, and then hooked his thumbs in her belt loops.

"I appreciate the passion. And that you're being rational about it. We've been pretending for months it wasn't happening."

She should step back, but the contact summoned memories she was tired of fighting. The reminder of how he tasted. His fingers digging into her skin when he was lost in the moment. Their bare bodies pressed together. Maybe this was a chance to make her apology about their past sincere. "Believe it or not, sometimes I'm willing to find common ground."

He gave a short laugh and tightened his grip on her hips. "I know I said a lot of things the other night, but I didn't mean to cast all the blame with you. I played just as much a part in fucking us up. Sometimes I'm even a little envious at your ability to just let go."

Odd statement. "I don't let go. I just hide it differently, and place value on different things."

"Sometimes I envy that too." He unhooked his thumbs from her belt loops and then nudged up the bottom of her shirt until his palms caressed her skin. "For instance, what were you two doing before reality interrupted the afternoon?"

She draped her wrists over his shoulders and intertwined her fingers at the base of his neck. A tiny voice whispered they were getting too intimate, but each touch and movement felt right. "Tetris."

"See? I couldn't do that."

She didn't know which struck her curiosity more—that he was expressing interest in how she spent her free time, or that he thought for some reason playing video games was off limits to him.

"Why not?"

He shrugged. "I fell behind that curve a long time ago. I suck at anything that requires a controller."

She wanted to laugh at the simple statement, but the serious crease in his brow made her suppress the impulse. "You ask me to aim any kind of digital weapon, and I get my ass kicked. It doesn't stop me from playing when I want."

He shook his head. "Like you said, we have different priorities."

"Like your ego?" There was no malice in the thought, and she hoped it didn't come off that way.

He shrugged. "Tell me your ego has never held you back from doing something."

His words should put her on edge, but the conversation didn't feel threatening. His comment was thought-provoking, but still casual. Like those talks they'd had when they were younger, that kept them out long past curfew, sitting on the grass in some park, wrapped in each other's arms. "It absolutely has, but that doesn't mean it's a good excuse."

He studied her for a moment. "If I told you that at the bar the other night, part of me really was hoping for another tumble, would you think less of me?"

Her skin burned under his hand, wanting more, and her imagination kicked into overdrive. The shift in subject caught her off guard, but it didn't feel forced. In fact, the suggestion was enticing. She tried to keep her tone light. "I didn't figure you were there for the crappy selection of on tap beer."

"I mean a tumble with you."

She started to tell him she doubted that, but it died in the back of her throat when she saw the sincerity in his expression. They were past swapping insults. She should pull away, but the thought wasn't enough to make her act. "You know this is a bad idea."

With his finger, he traced a line down her cheek to her jaw. "I don't know anything like that. I'm also not stopping you from leaving."

She didn't want to argue anymore. She was tired of the parrying and deflection and pretending not to notice how intense the spark between them was. The close, unguarded warmth jostled loose a memory she hadn't seen in ages—lunchtime on their first day of high school over a decade ago. All her friends were on a different schedule, and she'd found an isolated spot under a tree to eat alone. A guy, whose posture and gorgeous blue eyes radiated confidence, approached and floored her by asking if he could share her tree.

She'd accepted, and the next couple of years flowed from easy banter and people watching into something more. By the start of their junior year, it had been him with his back to the same tree trunk, and her sitting between his legs, his arms draped around her neck.

Something ached in Rae's chest as the memory faded but didn't vanish. She leaned into his touch. "I don't have anywhere else to be."

"Not that we're making a habit of this." He nipped her bottom lip with his teeth before he rested his forehead against hers.

She pressed closer, every inch of her screaming for more. A voice whispered through her mind that she'd make it a habit in an instant, if she thought she could get away with it. "Of course not. Stress relief, right?"

"Right. Sure." He ran his mouth along her jaw, down to her throat, and kissed along her collarbone. His voice was muffled. "I don't even care what we call it."

She ignored the implication that this might mean more. Falling for him almost destroyed her all those years ago, and that memory was at least as powerful as the good ones. But damn it, this felt right.

She tilted her head back with a sigh, closing her eyes, sinking into the sensations. He traced a line along her ear with his tongue and caught her earlobe between his teeth. The things that turned her on had shifted, become more refined, since back then. And he still managed to push a button—draw a new flare of pleasure—wherever he touched. She whimpered at the current that raced through her entire body.

"That sound does wicked things to me." His growl filled her head. He twisted his fingers in her hair and yanked her head back, his mouth finding hers. The sharp jerk spiked her desire. He kissed her hard, and she pushed back, teeth cutting into the inside of her lip. Hunger consumed her thoughts.

He turned them, so her back was to the couch, and nudged until her butt collided with it.

The power in his voice and strength in his grip were enticing and frightening at the same time. Not that Zach scared her, but her reactions to him bordered on terrifying. She struggled to close the door on her heart and still focus on the warmth of his mouth.

Her feelings burst through the gate and intertwined with her and the moment. Her mind complained that was bad. The rest of her let the emotion flow through her. It mingled with his touch. Heightened her response. Sang in her heart and along her skin. She pressed closer to him, memorizing every inch of his hard body pressed against hers.

She'd deal with getting over Zach later. Right now, feeling him was all that mattered.

chapter ten

It had taken the rest of Zach's self-restraint to play it cool when Rae showed up on his doorstep, passionate anger flashing in her eyes. His control evaporated the longer she stuck around. It probably wasn't the best idea to indulge this craving, but the last few months had worn on Zach, and if this was the one time he didn't have to hold back, he was diving into it.

He exposed her neck, and trailed his tongue down the soft skin. Her whimpers—in sharp contrast to the shell she wore when they argued—spurred him on. He wanted her now and wasn't in the mood to play anymore.

He dropped his hands to her waist and inched under her shirt. The sensation of skin on skin was satin temptation against his palms. Rae sighed and shifted her weight against him, every inch of her body rubbing against him through their clothes. That was an issue—too many clothes. His cock pulsed in agreement, already hard and straining against her hip.

He pulled on her top, and she took the hint and broke away long enough for him to yank it over her head. Red bra today. He scraped his teeth over her neck while he undid the clasp. *Fuck,* that was sexy. Her panties were probably cotton, mismatched, and had some kind of obnoxious screen-print on them.

He tossed her bra aside and trailed his lips down her chest. She arched her back, pushing closer. When his mouth wrapped around a swollen, pink nipple, her fingers dug into his scalp.

Every sound she made enveloped his thoughts. He flicked his tongue across her skin, his erection growing stiffer with each squirm and sigh. Reason told him to stretch the moment out, make it last, but reason was rapidly evaporating. It was hard enough not strip off the rest of her clothes right now, and drive his dick inside her. Feel her tight, wet pussy clench around him. Fuck her until he couldn't think.

She pulled his face back up, pressed her mouth to his, and caught his bottom lip between her teeth. Her brown eyes danced frantically over his face, searching for something. "At the risk of sounding crude…" She trailed her nails over the back of his neck. "I desperately want you inside me."

The request broke the last of his restraint. He was surprised he didn't tear something yanking her cutoffs open and pushing them to the ground. She tried to kick her shoes off, got tangled in her shorts, tripped, and landed with her palms flat on his chest.

"Sorry." She laughed, light and carefree.

He helped her balance while she stepped out of her sneakers and clothes, and toed both aside.

Hands on her hips, he lifted her to sit on the back of the sofa. He pushed between her legs. Something occurred to him, and he paused to drop his forehead onto her shoulder. He didn't want to lose this moment. Fuck.

"Something's wrong." Her pout was audible.

He looked at her again. He needed at least a hint of mental power to do this. Fortunately, not a lot. "Don't move?"

She gave him a hesitant smile. "Okay?"

"Condoms." *Night stand drawer, next to the bed.* It took more concentration than it should have to not trip in his sprint up the stairs. A moment later, he stepped back into the living room. She was still there, legs crossed at the ankles, every gorgeous curve exaggerated by her posture.

The creases in her forehead melted away when she saw him. He held up the foil package, and she shook her head with a tiny laugh.

"I suppose…" She wrapped her arms around his neck and her legs around his waist when he was within reach. "I should be grateful you don't have those stashed all over the house."

He stepped back enough to unzip his slacks, push the rest of his clothing to the ground, and then roll the rubber on. Her heat was rapidly erasing the ruined moment, tempting him again. "Your opinion of my sex life is a lot more interesting than the reality." He moved between her legs again. As he kissed up her neck, the scent of strawberries sank into his thoughts. "I've never even done it on this couch before."

"I get to be a first. I never would have guessed."

"I suspect a lot of things about me would surprise you." He positioned himself near her opening and nudged.

She sighed and tipped her head back. The pause to jog upstairs had given him just enough sense to take this at a more even pace. He entered her slowly, and her nails dug into his back. She moaned when he pulled out almost to the tip before thrusting back inside her again. The steady pace felt incredible, but he wouldn't have the patience to maintain it.

She shifted her weight against him, prompting him to increase the speed. He moved a hand to the small of her back to help her keep her balance and found her tit with the other. He pinched her nipple hard, and she ground against him in response. Each new squirm and sigh drilled into his head, making her the only thought in his mind.

She was so tight, so slick, and her cries short-circuited his thoughts. *Fuck*, this was all-consuming. Being inside her. A part of her. She rocked against him, picking up the already frantic rhythm. The clench around his cock strangled his reason.

The only thing that kept him from spilling inside her was the desire to see her get off. He wanted to see her get off though. That made the whole moment that much sweeter. He nipped her earlobe, voice strained. "Tell me what I have to do to make you come."

Her reply was breathless. "More of what you're already doing. Please don't stop."

At least that he could do. He slammed in harder, teetering on the edge of his own orgasm. His world spun as he held back. She scraped her nails down his back, and her legs tightened around him. Her breathing grew shallow.

Her pussy clenched, milking his cock as she

climaxed. She didn't let up, even as her moans slowed. The pounding rhythm coaxed him past his limits, and he grunted as he drove into her. The edge remained, even after he finished, slowly fading in a shower of sparks dancing across his vision. He slowed and then stopped, as the peak fell away.

She rested her forehead against his chest, and he dropped his head on her shoulder, both of them silent while they tried to catch their breath. His mind hadn't been this clear in a long time, and it had everything to do with the woman in his arms.

"Come on." He helped her stand, not able to hide his smile when she wobbled on her feet before finding her balance. He grabbed a tissue from a box on an end table to wrap up the condom and dispose of it.

He guided her to the other side of the couch, lay down, and patted the cushion in front of him.

She settled in, her back against his chest, and pulled his arm over her waist. "This is nice."

He propped himself up on one elbow to kiss along her shoulders and neck. "Definitely." Part of him was already looking forward to the next time. This was getting dangerous. *Do I care?*

The thought of selling everything and moving to New Zealand had taunted him for days. A way out. A chance to leave everything behind at forget this place. A pang in his chest said he didn't want to forget her, or what they shared. Would she go with him? He smothered the thought. He was tired of sinking his passions into anyone or anything. It only cost him in the end.

Silence drifted between them, and her breathing

slowed. He settled his palm on her stomach. "If you're going to fall asleep, my bed's more comfortable."

She leaned back into him with a sigh. That was amazing. He licked lightly along her soft skin, tasting the salt of perspiration and the strawberry scent of her shampoo.

"I was just thinking." Her voice was quiet, but distinct.

Not about them, right? Not the way he was. Not that he was thinking of them as a *them*. "That makes me nervous." He tried to keep the teasing in his tone.

Her arm dropped away from his, hesitation in her response. "You don't even know what it was about."

He wanted her back in the moment, wanted to spend the rest of the afternoon holding her and swapping inanities with her. He shouldn't entertain the idea, but the urge was undeniable.

"I didn't mean I don't like you thinking." He trailed a finger up her thigh to her hip and brushed the skin where leg met hip. "In fact, your thoughts are as sexy as the rest of you. But if your mind is already drifting, the distraction didn't work as well as it should have."

She relaxed again, full body pressing into him. "It worked fantastically, and now I'm thinking clearly."

"About?"

There was a long pause before she said, "I know how to make Cord work."

A surge of conflict slammed into his skull. He didn't want to have this conversation with her. A solution. Finally. Except letting someone he was sleeping with have a say in their company had already cost them everything once. He wasn't letting that line blur again, regardless of what she was about to say. Not that he was going to tell her that. He shifted his weight against her back. "Not the most seductive thing I've ever heard after sex."

"I'm serious." She let out a soft laugh, but it was laced with something heavier.

His enthusiasm and lingering glow were rapidly evaporating. "I'm a healthy, single man in my late-twenties. Getting laid *is* serious business."

She sat up, taking the throw with her, holding it in front of her chest. "Don't do this."

"Do...?"

She grabbed her shirt off the coffee table and put it on. "Don't play stupid. You could at least hear me out."

He was torn between keeping her there longer and not wanting to delve into something that would definitely send her away pissed. He sat up behind her and wrapped his arms around her waist. "I'm listening. Especially if you're talking dirty." That was probably the last thing he should say if he didn't want her angry.

A low sound that was something between a sigh and a growl vibrated through her chest and back.

He flopped back against the couch. "I'm listening."

"Promise?" She glanced over her shoulder, expression softening.

No, he wasn't giving in to that look. Even if it did gnaw at something deep inside. "Of course."

She relaxed a little more. "You start over."

All the pieces clicked together at once, as the meaning and consequences of those three words slammed through his thoughts. Starting over meant finding investors again, risking the same thing that happened last time: one of them screwing the company over.

And if it was her suggestion, it probably also meant getting her involved. After all, she specialized in making the numbers work, and she didn't the idea out there so they could let someone else do it.

"No." He slid away from her.

She shifted on the couch to face him completely, one leg tucked under the other knee, and her eyes narrowed. "You said you'd hear me out."

"Nothing to hear." He should have listened to the instinct that told him this was a mistake, and never for a moment indulged the part of him that thought he was falling for— No, wrong, that thought didn't exist. "If that was an option, we would have already done it."

"You don't know if it is or not. Just give me a few hours with your books—"

And there it was. "No." There was no way he was repeating what had happened with Kelly. "It won't work." He grabbed his clothes from the floor. This wasn't how he wanted this day to end.

She was on her feet in an instant, anger and hurt flashing in her eyes as she collected the rest of her clothing and yanked it on. "Tell me why not."

"Because it won't."

She clenched her jaw, staring him down. The moment stretched between them. She turned on her heel and stormed toward the door. The entire house shook when she slammed it behind her.

He sank back into the cushions. That had been painful, but it was the right thing to do. Thinking with his dick last time had cost them everything; he wasn't making that mistake again. Even if Rae hadn't been a fling. Even if they'd never slept together. Or dated. Or fantasized about the relationship becoming more…

Don't go down that road. Starting over isn't an option. He and Scott needed to sign the buy-out offers and move on.

chapter eleven

Zach dropped into the chair in his office, and air whooshed out through the seams in the leather. He rested his head on the cool glass of the desktop and took a deep breath. There was no reason to leave anything behind. He wouldn't be coming back. But the office had been his second home for so long. It was going to take more than a couple minutes to pack it all up.

Note to self—ask Legal if he was still entitled to the furniture, or if that was company property.

He came in early to clear out before anyone else got in, but reluctance made him drag his feet. Nostalgia was hitting him harder now he'd had a chance for everything to sink in. His focus drifted around the room, eventually falling on the table in the corner where he'd negotiated some fantastic deals, including hiring some of the most talented people in the industry.

He couldn't see the scratches in the polished walnut from where he sat, but he knew it was covered with them. More memories flashed through his mind. Talking to Scott about rehab. The night he and Kelly decided to test out how sturdy the furniture was.

The memory morphed, and it was Rae instead. Her legs wrapped around his waist. Her almost too-thin shirt shoved up, turquoise bra loose. The tiny sighs she made when she was content…

He shook his head to banish the thoughts. Maybe he wouldn't miss the table after all. It could stay and haunt the new management for all he cared. A knock drew him out of his thoughts. Scott claimed the chair across from Zach's desk. The familiarity of the moment brought a sad smile to Zach's face.

Scott looked around the room, gaze lingering on the modern art decorating the walls. "It'll look strange in here when you're gone."

"Not like you'll be around to notice." Zach didn't try and keep the bitter tone from his voice. It wasn't worth the effort, and Scott would know it wasn't directed at him. "You done packing up?"

"As much as you are." Scott slid down in the seat and settled his arms on the rests, legs sticking out in front of him. "I grabbed a couple of personal things. My laptop. I'll get the rest when they force me."

Zach frowned. The longer he lingered in the room, the more it settled in…it was all over. The only job he'd ever had. The only real one, anyway. What were they going to do now? People didn't actually retire at twenty-eight. How boring would that be? He dropped his forehead into his hand, shoulders slumping.

"Gentlemen." Vance's stern baritone sliced the lingering cloud in the room.

Swell. Is there even any reason to be civil at this point?

Scott shifted so he was half facing the door.

"I'm glad you're both here." Vance didn't wait for an invitation. He made himself comfortable in the empty chair next to Scott. "I was hoping to talk to you before my flight and before, well…"

Zach clenched his jaw. He'd put up with condescension from Vance and older businessmen like him for years without a problem. But this morning, it was the last thing he wanted to hear. *Pompous dickwad.* Zach kept the thought to himself, his forced smile growing bigger. "Have a seat." He let a hint of sarcasm slip into his offer. "We've got a few minutes."

Scott crossed his arms and sat up straighter, clamping his lips shut.

"Fantastic." If Vance sensed the hostility radiating in his direction, it didn't show. "The letter this weekend was so formal. I wanted to tell you both in person what a difficult decision these layoffs were for us. If we could have seen any way around letting such talented people go, we would have gone that direction instead."

The words felt hollow. Zach didn't like the tone or delivery. Was that what everyone they were about to fire would hear? Empty reassurances that meant nothing and held even less sincerity? Instinct told him not to burn this bridge. That wasn't how business operated. Wasn't how he operated. But almost half a decade of geezers telling him what he could and couldn't do was culminating in a single moment of frustration. He bit the inside of his cheek to measure his response. "I'm sure. Anything else?" Venom slid in anyway.

Scott's brow rose.

Vance didn't flinch. "I understand our Legal has agreed with your man on a final draft of the buyout offer. I'm sure you've signed by now."

Scott coughed.

Zach stood. He wasn't interested in salvaging this relationship. Not with the man who had spent the last twelve months threatening them, only to make real on those threats with cash. Not with the company who was forcing them away from something they'd built from the ground up. "We've got a couple more things to clear up here. Are you done?" Ice coated his words.

Vance smiled, not moving. "Throw your tantrum if you'd like. Get it out of your system. If those people are still working here in a week, they lose access to their severance offer. You wouldn't do that to them, would you?"

Where did that come from? Zach blinked, trying to shift to keep up with the new threat. "Our Legal—"

"Is going to get expensive if you're no longer working for the company retaining him." Vance cut him off. His phony smile vanished, and his eyes narrowed. "You're really going to pay out of your own pocket for a bunch of kids to fight a legitimate layoff? No wonder you're here now."

"We're here now"—Scott's angry exclamation was loud amid the quiet threats— "because you have some really shitty ethics. Those people out there deserve more than your callous brush-off and a form letter attached to a goodbye check."

Zach glared at him but didn't feel as much relief

as he wanted when Scott backed down with a scowl. There was a lot about this deal that didn't feel right, but technically there wasn't anything they could do now besides thump their chests.

Anger seethed under his skin, prickling his arms and making his muscles tense to the point his neck ached. He turned his attention back to the older man. "You're making some big assumptions about what we are and aren't doing."

"I assume nothing." Vance uncrossed his legs. "I know you haven't accepted our buyout offer yet. I know"—he gestured at the walls— "you haven't cleared out of here yet. I know I saw at least one person from the layoff list at her desk when I got here." He leaned forward, elbows resting on his knees. "Walk away now. You'll be under our roof long enough for our Legal to make sure all your paperwork is in order. You're a smart kid; I'm sure you'll make some sales team somewhere a lot of money."

Zach didn't know which infuriated him more: the knock against his age and skills, or the implication their lives would get difficult if they didn't just roll over and play nice. "I appreciate the advice." He stepped around the desk and stopped halfway to the door. "Now if you'll excuse us, we have *important* things to take care of this morning."

Vance smirked and stood. "Of course. It was great to get to know the staff last week. I'm sorry it wasn't under better circumstances."

Zach kicked the door shut after the him, dwelling on the twinge of disappointment it hadn't hit him in the ass. Fury gnawed at his senses, and he fought back the urge to punch the closest wall.

"We're fucked, aren't we?" Scott's angry question sounded distant. Desperate.

Zach took a deep breath, pushing back his rage and feeling it shift. Misery crawled through it. "Yes. No. I don't know. You done here for now? Let's get the fuck out of here."

Scott didn't move. "Because leaving the office at eight on a Monday morning for a stiff drink sounds like the best way to handle this."

"Exactly." Zach didn't know where the sarcasm was directed, or even how much of it was sarcastic and how much was sincere. He didn't care.

chapter twelve

Nervous energy thrummed through Zach. He tapped his fingers on the steering wheel and parked in front of the café. The white wrought iron, and candles on the middle of every table screamed *trendy*.

Every time he brought the buyout offer up with Scott, the conversation deteriorated into inaction. But Scott had extended the invite to lunch, so maybe they could reach common ground about why they needed to walk away from Cord now. That ought to take Zach's mind off Rae. Since she stormed out a week ago, her memory had moved into, and taken over, portions of his imagination…

The thought vanished when he saw the woman seated at a table outside, head bent close to Scott's, the two of them laughing about something.

God damn it, what was Rae doing there? He tried to pull his attention away from her. Her hair was in twin pigtails, leaving her neck exposed. Her opaque black T-shirt might have been a disappointment if it and her cutoffs didn't hug her curves perfectly. Besides, stripping the shorts off would solve the issue of what he could and couldn't see.

He cut off the fantasy before it could run rampant. At least he'd worn slacks; he hoped that would hide his reaction. Rae was done. In the past. If any of him thought otherwise, it was a bizarre reaction to the fact he got—no, *had*—to see her on a regular basis.

He dropped into the empty seat at the table. "Funny running into you here."

The pink in her cheeks darkened, and she ducked her head. That wasn't attractive. Or alluring. Or completely compelling and intoxicating. And the last thing he wanted to do was brush a thumb over her cheek and kiss her.

He pushed ice through his veins, wrapped in the word *Kelly*. He wasn't going to let his dick drive them into another business mistake. It didn't matter how badly he wanted Rae. That would pass.

"Not really." At least Scott sounded normal again. "I invited her."

Awesome. Fantastic. Why did Zach feel like he was being set up? He grinned, keeping his expression pleasant. "Epic. Anyone else coming?" The table wasn't big enough for more people, and there were only three chairs—he should have noticed that up front—so probably not. But the entire situation had him off balance, and he wasn't sure he could trust his instincts.

"Nah." Scott waved a hand. "I figured since we're all such great *just friends* now, we should hang out."

Rae winced, grabbed her water, and then took a long swallow. Condensation dropped from the glass.

It landed on her chest then trailed down between her breasts until it collided with her V-neck collar.

Zach forced his attention to Scott, searching for a hint of where the not-so-subtle dig had come from. "Just friends. Interesting qualifier."

"Not as interesting as you might think." A light quaver ran through Rae's voice. "My new contract doesn't start for two weeks, and apparently someone…" She glanced at Scott. "…has too much time on his hands. You suffering from the same thing?"

She'd found new work. That meant she'd be gone soon. An ache grew in his chest, clenching his heart like a vice. *Fuck.* Zach kept his gaze on hers. No need to let it drift elsewhere. His imagination was already doing enough of that. "No. I'm suffering from something entirely different."

She raised her brows and tilted her head to the side, the corner of her mouth pulling up.

He wouldn't lean in and kiss her light smile. He wasn't enticed by it. The faint scent of strawberries wasn't wreaking absolute havoc on his brain.

"I bet." Scott's tone was flat. "I'm surprised you haven't already booked a flight to Europe. Early retirement and all that."

Zach turned back to his friend. More hostility crept out with each comment. He didn't want to do this in front of anyone else, especially after the argument he'd had with Rae, but they needed to get over this. They'd lost, they needed to move on, and he wouldn't let Scott wallow. "I was thinking I'd start with Italy. If it's pretty, I might not come back. You made plans yet?"

Scott's knuckles went white around his glass. Out of the corner of his eye, Zach saw Rae drop her face in her hand.

You're being an ass.

If that was what it took to drive a wall between them, it was better for both of them in the long run.

"I thought I might not throw in the towel so easily." A sharp edge ran through Scott's voice.

This was bullshit. Zach was tired of dancing around it. He was irritated with himself for letting it go on so long, and Scott for not seeing they needed to stop pretending. "What are you going to do? Out of the five billion times we've had this conversation, what's your brilliant plan this time that you didn't have before?"

"I…" Scott faltered. "Something."

"Brilliant. Not one of your better ideas, but they can't all be best sellers."

"That's not fair." All the hesitation vanished from Rae's voice. The flush didn't look shy anymore. Her eyes were hard. "Your only solution is running away, so you don't have any room to talk."

And there it was—the reason he didn't want to do this here, in front of her. "And you've got a better plan?"

Shit. He shouldn't have asked that.

Her smile didn't reach her eyes. "Since you asked…"

"Wait, what?" Scott sat up straight. "You have an idea." He leaned in, anger evaporating in an instant.

"Wrong." Zach cut him off. "Remember Kelly?" Rae was actually doing this. She was going to hash out her painfully risky plan in front of the one person who would cling to any hope he could find, regardless of how unrealistic it was.

"The entire internet remembers Kelly." Rae's cold smile ate at him.

"Why is she here?" Zach asked Scott.

Scott shrugged, the hard set of his jaw softening a hint. "She asked if I was busy today. Said she had something she wanted to talk about."

A vein pulsed in Zach's eyelid as he watched the exchange. This was completely out of control. "What's going on?"

"We're listening to her idea," Scott said.

"No, we're not." Zach had his phone out. "I'm booking a one-way flight to another continent."

"Enjoy." Rae slouched in her seat, arms crossed and lips pursed.

Zach looked at Scott. "Come with me."

"What about Rae?"

Zach shrugged. "You don't really bring your ex-girlfriend on vacation with you." Each retort was measured, to be cruel and removed. And each word he spat out sliced deeper. He didn't want to do this. He *had* to do this. Experience dictated anything else was stupid.

Rae slapped the table as she stood, irritation running under her words. "This was a bad idea."

Zach's fingers twitched, and he had to grab his own leg to keep from reaching for her. When Scott wrapped a hand around her wrist, an unfamiliar surge of jealousy seared through Zach.

"Wait, please?" Scott said. "Don't listen to him. I want to hear what you have to say. Let him go whore around the Southern Hemisphere if he wants."

She crossed her arms, accentuating every curve the T-shirt hugged. Creases lined her forehead. "Yeah, no."

Zach forced his attention to stay on her face. Not her angry flush or bright kissable lips, but her piercing gaze. No, that wasn't working either. "Either sit or leave. People are staring."

"I'm not talking unless you're both listening." She rolled her eyes but dropped back into her chair.

Zach clenched his teeth, measuring his response. "Because your ego needs that kind of validation?"

Her narrowed eyes didn't hide the shimmer of almost tears. *Shit,* he shouldn't have gone there. He couldn't believe he'd thrown a private conversation—one about what parts of them they held back from the world of all things—back in her face.

She breathed through her nose. "Because—and so help me, I can't believe I'm saying this—it doesn't work without both of you."

"What doesn't?" Hope crept into Scott's voice.

She glanced up at the sky before turning back to him. "Starting over."

"Could we?"

"No." Zach hated the lift in Scott's question. This was all falling apart. They couldn't do this.

"Not if you're not both interested."

"Bad way to try and keep him in your life." Scott's voice had gone flat again.

Does he know? Zach's head swiveled toward his best friend, and out of the corner of his eye he saw

Rae's do the same.

"So neither of you wants to hear it." She was on her feet again. "That's fine. Honestly, I'm not sure there's room for both your egos anyway." She strode toward the parking lot.

"Rae, wait." Scott's plea hit her back.

She didn't turn her head once on her journey from the table to her car, and seconds later, she was peeling out of the parking lot.

"Nice. Glad she still only sees her side of things." Zach pulled his smokes from his pocket and bounced the pack on the table. The words hurt to say, but he needed to recognize the truth in them. It wasn't like he had anything to do with her reaction. Which was why he wasn't going to track her down and apologize. Much as every single inch of him hurt because he'd been the one to piss her off.

"You're one to talk. You couldn't even hear her out?" The venom was back in Scott's voice. "You're so fucking petty, you have to let personal issues come between you and a second chance?"

"There are no second chances." Not with her and not with Cord. "You can't do what we did and then try it again. We can't afford it on our own, and the moment we let investors in the door, we set ourselves up for this to happen once more. She doesn't know that. She doesn't see it. She's too busy trying to make everyone happy."

"No." Scott shook his head. "Not everyone. Besides, you know this is what she does, right? How she earns her living? If she thinks we can do it, do you really think spite is a good reason to ignore her?"

Zach was on his feet in an instant. He didn't

even know who he was pissed at anymore. "I think the fact it's a bad idea is a good reason to ignore her. I'm cashing out. If you don't want to do the same, don't throw my future away in the process."

Scott stood, back stiff and shoulders back, so his full height was obvious. His hands clenched into fists. It was an imposing posture, except Zach had seen it too many times to back down. Neither of them spoke for a moment. Scott finally plucked a twenty from his wallet and tossed it on the table. "She's right about one thing—there's not enough room for both of us in anything new."

And he was gone too, tearing out of the parking lot seconds after dropping into his SUV.

Zach rubbed his face. He didn't care. It was better this way. The words didn't devour him—not Scott's and not Rae's. Whatever they were clinging to, it wasn't healthy. Which was why he needed to completely ignore any urge to do the same.

chapter thirteen

Zach snubbed another smoke out in his ashtray as his car coasted to a stop on the freeway off-ramp. He leaned his head against the headrest, half paying attention to the red light and waiting for it to change.

How did things get so messy? Obviously the stuff with DM and Kelly were the start, and it had all gone downhill since then. Rae showing up in his war room looking for her sister's spare key was almost like a second catalyst. Not that he could blame her for the insider trading or shitty DM management.

He put the car into gear when the light changed and let his thoughts drift as he followed the road.

But Scott's stubbornness—that had to be all her. Even though he'd always been like that. She was trying to drive a wedge between them.

He changed lanes and turned at empty intersections, enjoying the path of least resistance option for going nowhere.

Rae had even used Scott to back him into a confrontation in order to be heard.

Zach ignored the nagging voice whispering he would have done the same to get his own way and had on several occasions. There wasn't a comparison.

What Rae was talking about was financial suicide. At least Kelly had had investment capital.

The last thing he needed was to rehash how everything having to do with Kelly was a bad idea. That always led to regret and comparisons with Rae and then the fantasies.

He licked his lips, suddenly realizing how dry his mouth was. He popped the glove compartment open. No gum. He pulled his car into the first parking lot he came to. The shopping center was almost deserted. A single shop was open, tucked away between two abandoned store fronts.

Recognition whispered through him, and he realized he knew this strip mall. He spent a lot of time there in high school. With Rae. There was no way it was the same place. There had never been any customers back then. The sign was the same, but it had probably just been cheaper to keep it when ownership changed.

Part of him didn't like the idea of stepping back into that memory, but he was thirsty, and pride refused to let anything to do with her drive his decisions. Besides, once he stepped through the front door, he could close that part of his past. *Because that's worked out so fantastically for you lately.* The sarcasm in his own words rubbed his thoughts raw.

A bell on the handle jangled when he entered the shop. It took his eyes a moment to adjust to the dim lighting.

"Evening," a cheerful voice called from the counter. "What can I get you tonight?"

He wasn't looking at the coffee shop employee. His gaze had been drawn to the back of the room and a familiar booth.

No.

Rae stared back, cheeks puffy. She blinked, brown eyes a melancholy compliment to the red rimming them.

Zach needed to leave. *Closure zero. Getting stuck in the past wins.*

"Do you need a minute?" the barista asked.

"He'll have an Italian soda with cherry." Rae's voice was clear and empty in the otherwise deserted room. She stayed seated, but never looked away from Zach.

"Half and half?" the barista asked.

Rae shook her head. "No. The cream makes the cherry taste funny."

Zach wasn't sure what compelled him forward, but he found himself sliding into the seat across from her. The joke tickled something in the back of his mind. Something he didn't want to enjoy. He'd always teased her about it when they were dating. He'd loved to see her blush when he made the comment about the cream and the cherry and winked at her.

That had been more than ten years ago. So much had changed since then.

The barista set the drink in front of him.

Zach handed him a five. "Keep the change."

"Thanks, man."

Zach didn't touch the drink. Thirsty didn't seem important anymore. His mind was moving so quickly, he couldn't grasp anything. He wasn't used to being at a loss for words.

"Let's try this again." Rae finally broke the

silence. "Why are you so dead set against my idea?"

"It's not—"

She held up her hand. "No, that's how the conversation went last time. That won't work. How about this? I'm not Kelly."

The sorrow in her eyes called to something inside him. Zach fumbled for a response. "So I noticed."

Her cheeks dimpled for a moment before the half smile vanished again. "Are you sure? That night you rescued me at the bar… The conversation we had in the car after... I've replayed that in my head so many times since then."

Don't let her do this. He didn't want to linger on those memories. It wasn't relevant, and it wouldn't solve anything. "And?"

"You told me our breakup hurt because what we had together was different than what you had with anyone else. Together, we were unique."

No. Unwanted emotion bubbled up inside. He wasn't going to listen to this. "We're talking business. Don't make it personal."

She took a deep breath, and her expression went blank again. "At the risk of sounding immature, you started it. This isn't about the fact we had great sex, or that I still wish I hadn't walked away from my perfect guy back in high school. And you know what? This *is* personal. It doesn't matter if we try and pretend otherwise. I wouldn't be upset if I didn't care, and neither would you."

She took a sip of her coffee, grimaced, and then pushed the cup aside. "I don't know why Kelly did what she did to the two of you. I don't know why you and she didn't work out. I do know it wouldn't have been possible if she hadn't had controlling interest in your company."

"So we're back to casting blame."

She clenched her hands, knuckles whitening. Her tone remained even. "No. Not even close."

He shouldn't be picking this fight. He needed to hear her out. But she was reopening so many old wounds. "Are you sure?"

"If you'd listen for a minute, you'd know." She slid down in her seat, fists loosening. Crescent-shaped creases marred her palms where she'd dug her fingernails in.

He wanted to bury it all under an argument, but he couldn't drag enough fight to the surface. "You talk, I'll listen. No assumptions."

"I loved you back in high school."

He swallowed as the unexpected words—the phrase he lived to hear back then—sank in.

She didn't look at him. "I didn't know how to act in a relationship. I'm not saying I'm an expert now, but I have a better idea of what not to do. I would have done anything to keep you."

"You broke up with me. Left town without even saying goodbye." He wished the retort had come out with less emotion behind it.

She raised an eyebrow. "Told you I didn't know what I was doing. You're going to insist you acted perfectly?"

"You know I'm not saying that."

"I'm not suggesting this solution because I'm looking for some sort of sick and twisted vengeance. I don't like the way things went, but those memories define me, and they remind me not to be that person.

It's also not what's driving me to offer my help." She locked her gaze on him, dark eyes sincere. "Unlike Kelly, my stake in this isn't financial. I'm not going to charge you for the idea. I don't expect you to give me a third of any of the results. I'm doing it because the two of you are talented and good together, and you got screwed. You deserve another chance…"

She trailed off, studying her fingernails. "Anyway. It doesn't matter. If you're not interested, I'll drop it. It's your decision. No pent up resentment because we don't agree. No telling people how much you suck."

"No spending the next decade wondering what you did wrong?" He didn't know if he was asking her if that's what she'd done, or admitting his own regrets.

Her eyes shone when she looked at him. "I can't promise that, Zach."

She stood.

His resolve broke. He couldn't let her walk out with their only solution they had because of spite. He couldn't let her walk out, period. Scott was right; Zach needed to stop comparing Rae to Kelly. There were no similarities between the two women except their intelligence. Zach was guilty of every single thing he held against her.

And having her around—hanging out, swapping stories, ideas, and gropes—was amazing.

He grabbed her hand and pulled her back down on the bench next to him.

Her knee brushed his leg, and she stared at him,

eyes wide.

This was business. The electricity between them was pleasant, but if he was going to do this—if he was going to ask for her help—it couldn't be because he was still attracted to her. "Do you really think we can start over?" Quickly, he added, "The company?"

"I'm not certain. I have to see both your finances. I promise I don't plan on anyone living off ramen, but there would be a significant shortage of five star steakhouses in your future."

"Do I get to keep my car?" He tried to sound light-hearted about it. The car was his pride and joy. He'd paid cash for it back before they really made it.

Rae smiled, dimples coming back. "Possibly longer than you were planning on. No promises, but if you can follow a budget both professionally and personally, I can probably make it work."

An impulse raced through him. The last thing he needed to do was kiss her. Instead, he grabbed his drink. Condensation dribbled onto the table. He took a long swallow, ignoring the watered-down result from all the ice melting.

She ducked her head again and scooted back on the bench, putting a few inches between them.

He tried to fight the ache it summoned. "I'll make things better with Scott." It was his fault anyway, for being a stubborn ass. "Are you free tomorrow?"

"I—umm…"

"To work through this with us. I mean, we'll pay you a standard consulting fee or something. We'll give you everything you need." He was rambling. He snapped his mouth shut.

Something in her expression shifted. "I'm not doing it for money."

"I didn't mean that, but this is your job. I just…" Was he really willing to beg for this? For something he wasn't even sure he wanted? Except he did want it. "Please?"

She nodded and stood again. "I've got time. I was supposed to do something with Scott, but… Things are kind of awkward right now."

Zach wanted to brush away her sad smile, but if this was business now, he had to keep it business. "Something tells me it'll be okay. I'll pick you up at, like…eight? You're still a morning person, right?"

She smiled. "Yeah. But I can meet you there."

He shook his head. This was one place he was confident: making the situation look right. "We show up together. That way Scott knows we're both on board."

She looked like she wanted to protest, but instead shouldered her purse. She extended her hand. "Deal."

He shook it, trying not to sink into the pulse that rushed through him at her touch.

chapter fourteen

Zach couldn't ignore the scuff of Scott's socks on carpet. The pacing had gotten old hours ago.

Rae stretched her hands over her head, her yawn ending in a squeak. Three displays—her laptop and the two she had commandeered from Scott and Zach—cast a series of sickly glows across her thin top. "Sit down, please?" She rubbed her eyes, muffling her voice.

"That won't do you any good." Zach propped his feet up on the coffee table. It took restraint to keep his eyes on the TV and not on her. But it was all because he was worried about the numbers she was pulling. It had nothing to do with the way her shirt curved over her tits when she stretched, or the arch of her back as she tried to work the kinks out of her neck.

Whatever had been exploding on TV stopped, and he changed the channel. A new flame-inspired concussion tore from the subwoofer, and Scott jumped.

"Seriously, dude." Zach tossed a couch cushion at him. "The people below you have to hate you."

"Whatever." Scott shoved his hands in his

pockets and stopped pacing. His toe tapped against the carpet.

"I'm done." Rae spun in the chair in front of Scott's desk. She rolled her head, stretching out her neck.

"And?" Scott was next to her in an instant, looking over her shoulder.

"That's the best I can do for you." She gestured at the screen. "You two have to decide if you can work with that."

Zach joined them, standing behind her. A series of spreadsheets with numbers stared back. He recognized the labels, but that didn't mean they made any sense. He was as unsuccessful translating Rae's work as he was trying to ignore the whisper of her strawberry shampoo. "Point us in a direction."

She grabbed the mouse and clicked one cell after another. "Each of these numbers links back to a tab. They tell you how much you can spend on salaries, advertising, office rental, all of it, and how I got those numbers. This will keep you solvent for eighteen months. You'll have to start turning a profit by then, or mortgage a house. There are some suggestions in there about things like pre-orders and online monetization to help you meet the goal."

As she explained, the figures started to make sense to Zach. "What if we take a pay cut?"

She rubbed a spot between her neck and shoulder. "You could, but I wouldn't recommend it. I've given you enough to pay your bills and still have some fun. If you cut yourselves off too completely, you'll be miserable and start to wonder if it's worth it."

"Not going to happen. It's worth it." Giddiness ran rampant through Scott's words. "So we can really do this?"

"Yes." It was the first time she'd given them a direct, positive answer.

Zach rested his hands on her shoulders, thumbs kneading into her neck. Her skin was soft under his fingers, and she relaxed as he worked almost unconsciously on a knot. He realized he was leaning closer, and moved his head back again. "You're brilliant. I'm sorry I doubted you. One more question. Okay, more than one, but one to start."

Scott looked at him, something marring the joy in his eyes.

Rae sighed and leaned back into the massage. She closed her eyes. "Sure."

Zach nodded at the screen, even though she couldn't see it. "That number there…next to office space."

She opened one eye long enough to look at the screen again. "That's based on what you pay now, with a bump in rent for inflation. You probably don't need as big a space to start, so you should be able to make it work."

"I'm not worried about that." Zach knelt next to her. Heat flowed between them.

Scott sniffed and took a step closer.

Rae's entire body went rigid, and she sat up, pulling away. "Okay?"

Zach's frown vanished almost as soon as it appeared. "If we didn't have to pay rent, could we get another employee?"

She stood and moved aside, gesturing for

someone else to sit in the chair. "Yeah, depending on what you wanted them for. But I already took into account everyone you told me you needed."

Zach rested a hand on her arm and turned her so they were face to face. The only sound in the room was the whir of computer fans. A large explosion burst from the surround-sound system, and everyone jumped.

"If we set the whole thing up—oh, say—in my basement, could we afford you?" Zach asked.

Scott's eyes grew wide as he studied Rae. "Good call."

She took a step back from Zach, looking between him and Scott. "I… I mean… Me?"

Scott's posture shifted, shoulders relaxing, hands resting in his pockets.

Good. No one was on edge anymore. Zach slid into the chair and began clicking through tabs and numbers too fast to be looking at them. "Of course you. This is your plan. You've got experience. Is eliminating the building rental enough to buy you away from contracting? Because we'd want you full time."

"I can't— I mean, I didn't…"

Zach whirled in the chair and grabbed her hands between his. He told himself it didn't matter how delicate her fingers were or how soft her skin felt. That wasn't what this was about.

She pulled away as if she'd been shocked.

He didn't flinch, but something inside snarled at the recoil. "You say we can do it, right?"

"Right…"

"You're confident enough in us, you'd let Chloe

sign on again," Zach said.

Rae nodded slowly.

"Confident enough you'd let both of us blow an early retirement on it." Zach told himself it was all about proving her numbers. If she wasn't certain enough in them to take a job, they weren't solid numbers. It had nothing to do with keeping her around longer.

"Neither of you would have been happy retiring anyway." The look on her face didn't give away whether or not she figured out the line of questions yet.

"That's not what he asked." Scott must understand where the conversation was headed. "If the numbers are good, and you think we can do it, you don't have anything to lose."

She stared at Scott. "Yes. There's enough there to buy me away."

Scott grinned. "We'll have you an offer letter on Monday."

Her smile was more hesitant. "Sounds like a blast. Do I get a spiffy title like the two of you have?"

"You want something better than—what was it Vance called you? Unemployed?" Scott's tone was teasing.

"Chief Financial Officer." Zach didn't know where that had come from. Even though they'd let Kelly invest back in the day, she'd always been a silent partner. Why was he willing to give this woman so much trust, less than twenty-four hours after insisting she was insane?

It was a bit much to prove a point, but it was too late to take it back now. Zach looked at Scott.

"You're okay with this?"

Scott only paused for a second. "Sounds perfect."

Zach was on his feet again. He grabbed Rae's hand. "So, listen. We have this friend, right?"

Rae stared blankly at him.

"And she just got this fantastic job offer, and we want to take her to celebrate."

Scott laughed.

Rae's mouth twisted, but she didn't successfully hide her smile.

Zach ignored both. "That's in the budget, right? Because there's no way we're letting her pay."

Rae ducked her head and tucked a strand of hair behind her ear. Her reply was soft, laced with laughter. "I think it'll be all right. Just this once."

Zach led her toward the door. He glanced over his shoulder at Scott. "That place downtown?"

Scott didn't hesitate. "The Italian one?"

Zach nodded. "Kelly always said they had good wine." He expected something inside to cringe at the reminder, but the lingering hurt was gone.

Zach glanced sideways before turning his attention back to the road. As dinner had worn on, Rae grew more and more quiet, eventually pulling away from the entire conversation. When they'd said good night and Scott had hugged her, she'd looked like it was taking all of her restraint not to bolt from the room.

She had given single word answers to Zach's questions on the drive to Chloe's, and spent the rest of her time sliding her watch up and down her wrist. When she spoke, her soft request echoed in the quiet car. "Tell me something?"

Anything, as long as it got rid of the awkward silence. "Sure."

"Why the change of heart?"

He hadn't expected her to dwell on his earlier reluctance to listen to her idea. She'd gone along with everything, so he assumed she was okay with it. He stalled as he tried to think of a reasonable response. "About?"

She blew a strand of hair out of her eyes. "About my plan. You were almost violently opposed to it, and now you're treating it like it's the most precious thing in the world."

What was a good answer? *Shit.* He shouldn't be stalling. Why couldn't he come up with something clever? Because he didn't want to lie. Not to her.

She shook her head. "So you really were doing it because of me."

How did she know that? "No, of course not."

"Really?" She flopped back, skull slamming into the headrest with a *thunk*. "So if Scott had come up with the idea, you would have been just as opposed. Or Jordan?"

No. "Of course." He couldn't hide his cringe at the taste of the lie. "Look, I'm sorry. I just… We got burned once before."

"By a different awkward little girl?"

"I realized I wasn't being fair to you. It's why I swallowed my pride. I'm glad I did."

He parked in front of Chloe's building. How was he going to make this better?

She twisted sideways in her seat, hands on the armrest between them, face inches from his. The coffee she'd had at dessert hung heavy on her breath, mingling with the strawberry shampoo he couldn't help but associate with her. Her lips were close enough for him to feel their heat, but she never touched him.

Holy fuck. He wanted her. The revelation struck him hard, throbbing in his head and lower down.

Her voice was a whisper. "If you think you can win me over by feigning interest in my ideas, if you think that's how I tick... That it's the best way to get me into bed... You're wrong."

He kept his expression impassive, eyes searching hers. It wouldn't hurt him to be a little honest. "They're two separate things." The low tone of his voice matched hers, his lips hovering millimeters away. "How much I want you has nothing to do with whether or not you've got a good idea."

When she pulled away, something inside him crashed and disintegrated.

She opened her door, and warm air wafted in to mingle with the air conditioning. "I can't pinpoint why, but I'm not sure I believe you. Maybe it's because you're still not telling me everything."

He wasn't letting the conversation end like this. He rested a hand on her arm. "It wasn't easy for me to admit why letting you do this scares me. Give me some leeway."

She sighed and leaned her head back against the seat. "Where do we draw the line? Are we colleagues? Lovers? You don't want to lose everything, and I don't want that either. But if they're two separate things, as you keep insisting they are, how are we going to keep from clashing?"

He didn't want to think about the questions, but he adored her for asking. That didn't give him any answers, though. "We figure it out along the way?"

"Do you think that's going to work? What if we can't figure it out? If our screwing ends with us hating each other, there are consequences that extend beyond us. That's what you're worried about, and it's a valid concern."

"So what do we do about it? You have an idea, I assume?" He didn't want to let irritation leak into his question, but his frustration at not having answers had reached its limit. "We don't see each other anymore outside the office? How well do you think that's going to go?"

"We have to dial things back." She slid her watch up and down her wrist, not looking at him. "The sex was about closure and stress relief, right? We got that. Can we figure out how to just be friends instead?"

It wasn't that he disliked the idea of friendship with Rae, but he wanted that on top of everything else, including her. Except, she had a good point. "Yeah. Friends is a good idea."

She climbed from the car, still not meeting his gaze. "See you tomorrow." Her voice was so quiet, he had to strain to hear the words. She strode toward Chloe's apartment without another glance back.

This was the right decision. So why did it make him clench his teeth and want to slam his fist into the dashboard?

chapter fifteen

Rae lay on her mattress, staring at the ceiling. Sleep wasn't coming. Why did she have to go and apply logic to something like emotion? She promised herself she wouldn't let him get under her skin. That she could walk away. That, with enough distraction, he would barely be more than a flicker in the back of her mind.

So why can't I get him out of my head? And why do I feel guilty for pushing him away the way I did?

Because she was so focused on not getting attached, she was ignoring all the important details: how much she enjoyed talking to him, the small gestures that made her pulse race almost as much as his kisses did, and just spending time with him. When had keeping their relationship physical become an all-encompassing motivation for her?

Without getting out of bed, she grabbed her phone off the nightstand. The glare of the screen was harsh in the dark room, and she winced until her eyes adjusted to the glow. There was no way she could say what she needed in a single message, but she had to tell him something. She couldn't leave things the way she had. She deleted and restarted her text several times before settling on a simple message.

I was wrong.

He wasn't going to answer tonight. She might as well get some rest.

The minutes dragged by. Her brain still wouldn't shut up. Giving up on sleep, she climbed out of bed. She pulled on a pair of knit shorts, straightened her camisole, and then made her way into the kitchen. Chloe's bedroom door was closed, and the flicker of pale light coming from underneath, but lack of sound told Rae her sister was gaming with her headphones on rather than having fallen asleep with the TV on.

A quiet knock filled the dark room, sending a tremor through Rae, and she paused. She swallowed and padded toward the door. Her heart flipped when she peered through the peephole. Zach stood on the other side, tugging on his ponytail.

She flipped the deadbolt off and opened the door enough to let him in. He took the silent offer and stepped inside, kicking the door shut behind him. He brought his hands to her face, cupped her cheeks, and then kissed her. There was hunger in his lips. It stole her breath as he held her close, and she gasped when they broke apart. He studied her, blue eyes hungry.

She didn't know what else to do. She pressed her frame against him and crushed her mouth to his. The sensations set her nerve endings on fire, and she stumbled back, pulling him with her. She hit the arm of the couch, lost her balance, fell backward, and landed on the cushions.

He laughed as he kneeled on the couch,

straddling her, and brushed a loose strand of hair out of her eyes. "I couldn't sleep. I was out driving, and I got your message, and I… I don't even know. I had to see you."

"What are we doing?"

He shook his head. "Not talking. For God's sake, we've done enough of that." He leaned forward, lips brushing her collarbone then tracing a line up her neck. "We can hash it all out later, I promise, but, holy fuck, I want you so bad right now—and we can talk if you want, but I don't promise I'm thinking clearly."

She arched her back and moaned as his lips roamed her skin. "Later is good for me too."

He slid his hand down her side, under her shirt, and then back up her spine. He shifted his weight, pressing his rock hard cock against her hip.

A voice whispered in the back of her head. *This is the other extreme end of the spectrum from the no-strings sex we've had up till now.* Even though they were saving the conversation about details, after the words exchanged in the car she knew this meant more. Was *more* what she really wanted?

The only thing she'd ever gained from over-analyzing her relationship with Zach was a headache. She wanted this. She wanted him. An annoying inner voice wasn't going to take it from her.

She crushed her mouth against his. Their tongues danced around each other, probing and massaging.

His leg slipped, and he broke away long enough to find a new position on the sofa.

She slid from underneath him, enjoying the

question in his eyes. Heat spread through her cheeks at her own boldness. She nodded toward the bedroom. "If you want, we could do this somewhere with a little more privacy and room to maneuver."

He helped her stand, and his lips glided along her ear. "I want."

She led him toward the bedroom, boldness battling doubt. Uncertainty took control for a moment, and she hesitated.

He didn't seem deterred. He sat on the edge of the mattress and pulled her down next to him. The hungry way he pressed his mouth to hers chased away her questions, and buoyed her emotion to the surface. This was incredible. He leaned her back, never pulling his lips away. Her heart clenched and skipped.

He followed the curve of her breast with his hand, fingertips trailing up to the rigid point. When he brushed his thumb across the swollen nub, she gasped at the pull that ran through her. He pinched the pink button, twisting and pulling. "Harder," she pleaded.

He obliged. "You're sexy as fuck. In case I haven't specifically said that yet."

The words mingled with his touch and raised her temperature. She dug her nails into his back when he found a sweet spot. Taking the cue, he shoved her tank top out of the way and lowered his lips to suck her nipple— alternating between a flicking tongue and light nibbles. Her senses flared to life, dancing around each new sensation. Everything she'd tried to force with Scott flowed to the surface now. Need. Passion. Desire.

His attentions left her head feeling as if it was full of helium. She took her camisole off and nudged his shoulders. She wanted to taste him.

"What are you up to?" he asked as he rolled onto his back.

"You'll see." She moved between his legs, spurred forward by the bulge underneath. The denim of his jeans was rough but pleasant against her thighs. She moved her lips across his chest. She said a silent *thank you* when she didn't fumble too much with his belt or zipper.

She kissed down his chest to the newly exposed skin. He moaned when her cool fingertips found his warm member through the fabric. She met his eyes as she freed him, and wrapped her hand around his shaft. She flicked her tongue over the swollen head. He closed his eyes and inhaled sharply through his teeth.

"Later." He reached down and drew her up to lie next to him.

"What guy doesn't want a blow job?"

He propped himself up on his elbow and traced lines along her bare stomach. A smile played on his lips. "I do, trust me, I do. But honestly, I won't hold out long with your soft lips wrapped around my cock, and I want to hear you scream first."

A sharp stab of arousal filled her at the blunt confession, but she tried to stay coy. "Scream, huh? My sister's in the next room."

"Wearing her headphones, music all the way up. I know my people. Can we focus on us again?" His warm palm on her stomach and lips pressed to hers pushed the concern aside. His hand slid lower, brushing the outside of her thin shorts, and her hips shifted closer to his touch. He rubbed her mound through fabric with his fingers, and his erection pressed into her leg.

He trailed his mouth down her jaw and then back to her neck. His touch dipped under the elastic waist of her panties to the smooth flesh beneath. She bit her bottom lip in anticipation.

He dipped his fingers between her folds. "You're so wet. You're not enjoying this, are you?"

"Maybe." Meant to be sultry, her reply came out as a shy whisper.

She sighed and tilted her head back when he found her clit. Her hips ground against his hand, and he pushed harder. Her breathing became shallow gasps, and she gripped the comforter. Pleasure spread through her body, filling her fingers, tingling in her breasts, clenching in her belly. When she let herself feel everything, not just the physical, but the affection and adoration—all of it—each new touch flared on a whole new level.

She thrust her hips up to get closer to his touch, and to keep from getting too loud, bit the inside of her check until it throbbed. Her eyes clenched shut at the swelling waves inside her, telling her she was close. Disappointment and hurt washed over her when he stopped just short of the finish line. Her mouth twisted, and she peered at him through one eye.

"Don't pout. Well, maybe just a little—it's cute on you." He stood and discarded the remainder of his clothing before he grabbed her shorts.

She lifted her butt off the bed long enough for

him to pull off her shorts and panties. He reclined next to her, cock pressing into her leg.

His lips hovered over her ear again, fingers tracing lines along her stomach and chest. "I want you on top of me." He grabbed her wrists as he rolled onto his back.

She didn't follow. She wanted to, but something stopped her.

It was his turn to look disappointed. "What?"

She hated responsibility. He'd always handled it before. Maybe she should have picked up condoms herself, but it wasn't as if she'd expected to make this a habit. Hoped, maybe, but not expected. Did Chloe have any? Not in plain view, and Rae felt awkward about digging through her sister's belongings. "I don't have any condoms."

"I'm clean."

Good line. Not a new one, but he pulled it off better than most guys. She tried not to be self-conscious of sitting in front of him naked. It didn't work. She crossed her arms over her bare boobs. "Doesn't matter."

He sat up next to her and kissed her. "I adore how stubborn you are." Never leaving the bed, he reached down, grabbed his wallet from his jeans, and then plucked a foil square from the battered tri-fold.

Rae didn't know if she should be amused or bothered that he was not only prepared, but had pretended otherwise. That's right, she wasn't thinking too much.

Wrapped up, he pushed her shoulders. She fell back, and he forced her legs apart with his knee. Excitement spilled through her, swirling and dancing in her thoughts. He leaned in and kissed her earlobe, his breath warming her skin. "I guess I'll have to get the mood back now."

He traced his tongue down her throat, and she arched her back. He hooked his hands under her knees and moved forward, his moan mingling with her whimper when he entered her. The penetration drove any negative thoughts aside and drew her back into the now. Being under him, wrapped around him, a part of him, felt so right.

He thrust against her in a slow rhythm, pulling almost all the way out before plunging deep again. Every time he thrust, an intense spark raced through her. She shifted closer, moving her hips faster and hoping he'd take the hint.

He gasped. "If you do that, I won't last long."

He'd already coaxed her so close to climax, her body just needed a little more of a nudge. She bit her bottom lip, response breathy. "I don't care."

He followed her cue, pounding against her and matching her need. A powerful surge built inside her. Her moans grew louder. Something in the back of her mind reminded her to keep it down. Geez, this felt incredible. Her inner muscles clenched around him, and orgasm rushed through her.

Still riding the waves of her climax, she heard him grunt, and he thrust his pelvis against her. His hands slid to her hips, his frantic pace slowing and then stopped.

He leaned forward to kiss her deeply before he rolled to the side to lie next to her on his back.

She struggled to catch her breath as she rested her head on his shoulder and her hand on his chest.

The only word she could find was a soft *mmm*.

He moved a hand to the small of her back, holding her close. "Now we can talk." His words vibrated through her palm and cheek.

She smiled against his skin. "Nope. No words. Sorry."

He traced a finger along her shoulder blade with his other hand. His quiet voice drifted through the dark room. "You know I'm sorry about what I said the other day, right? I really enjoy hearing what you're thinking."

The apology sent a new type of warmth rushing through her to blend with the euphoria. He meant the argument at his place. Even though the brush-off had dug deeply, she'd almost forgotten about it with everything that had happened over the last few days. "It's not a big deal."

"It is to me." His chest sank when he exhaled. "Here's the thing… You probably don't remember, but way back in the day, when our biggest worries were passing tests and whether or not we all had enough change in our pockets to put gas in someone's car, we used to sit under that stupid tree."

Her smile grew. She kissed his chest. "I loved that tree."

He intertwined his fingers with hers, their hands resting on his ribs. "I used to count the minutes until lunchtime, partly because I was a teenage boy, and I knew the sexiest girl in school was going to climb into my lap."

She flushed at the description and the way it loosened the memory, blended the feelings of then into now.

He tilted his head up enough to kiss her on the forehead, and then flopped back onto the pillow. "But at least as much because we always had the best conversations. No one sees the world the way you do, and you don't mind making that clear."

She melted into him, not sure what to say. He remembered and enjoyed their time in high school the same way she did and for the same reasons.

The revelation sank deep until it nudged something loose. A whisper of fear. A pit she didn't want to acknowledge. Did that mean they were about to make the same mistakes as before? *No.* She'd learned her lesson, and they knew their limits. They were talking things through—that definitely didn't seem to be a problem anymore. They'd be fine.

chapter sixteen

"You want me to build a no-room-for-error development calendar for the next nine months?" Scott sounded irritated, and his bunched up eyebrows reinforced it. "I don't usually do this for more than a couple of weeks at a time."

They were gathered at Chloe's. She refused to hang around when Zach and Scott were over discussing work—said it was too false-hopey for her—so she was at Jordan's.

"You have to know it's possible." Rae needed to remember that, even though these men were her friends—she glanced at Zach—and more, they were still her clients. Colleagues? They weren't being difficult on purpose. She just had to make them understand, and at the moment, that centered around Scott proving on paper he could meet the aggressive development schedule he'd laid out without burning his developers out.

"Don't be unrealistic," she said. "But be aggressive. Look at what your people can do on a deadline versus what they do when that pressure isn't there, and find a spot somewhere in the middle."

Scott sank back into her couch. "What makes

you think they don't produce the same amount of work all the time?"

She stared back at him, lips pursed.

He laughed. "I'm not the only one working, right? You're going to make him do something?"

"Absolutely." She looked at Zach, trying to ignore the heat lurking beneath his disinterest. The three of them were finalizing plans before they started making job offers and announcing their new venture. She was doing what she did with any company, making them prove they could work within the numbers she'd mapped out. "He's going to go through his address book and see if he knows anyone who wants to invest."

She could have sworn the temperature in the room dropped fifty degrees in an instant. Scott coughed, and Zach glared at her.

"Not funny." Zach's words held a hard edge.

She'd mentioned investors seriously once, and met such a hostile response she'd immediately crossed it off their list. Neither of them wanted to end up in the same situation again, and she didn't blame them. She held up her hands. "Okay, I won't tell that joke again."

Zach relaxed.

Scott rolled his eyes. "And if you're holding one back about sleeping with the boss, cross that off your list too."

Her eyes grew wide. Right. There was that. The secret he didn't know yet.

Zach gave her an almost imperceptible shake of his head before responding. "You know something I don't, man? What happened to just friends?"

Scott looked up. Zach stared back. Scott flinched first. "Nothing happened to it. Aren't you doing something?"

Rae forced herself to breathe and make sure she could keep the nervous waver from her voice before she spoke. "He's calling people. Hardware distributors, benefits companies, anyone he's ever met, or who he thinks might know his name, and making sure he can get you the best deals possible."

"On it, boss." Zach was already pulling his phone out and wandering into her room. Seconds later, the door swung shut behind him.

"You know." Scott didn't look up from his screen. "A month ago I would have sworn you'd rather die than let him in your bedroom, even a temporary one."

She laughed. Did that sound as forced as it felt? "Funny how things change."

"Hmm. True." He tapped a few more things in. "What happens if there are people who don't accept our job offers?"

Relief nudged her at the change in topic. This she could do. "There will be."

He frowned.

"It happens," she added quickly. "You're a startup. They've already been burned once, and some people will get better offers. But you do what you did last time: find the undiscovered talent and let them shine. You're building from the ground up, so proprietary knowledge doesn't mean anything except being comfortable with each other."

"That's worth a lot." He gave her his full attention. "You get a couple of people who bounce off each other just right, and suddenly everything moves faster. Kind of like with you."

She dropped onto the couch next to him. "How so?"

He shrugged. "You and I operate on the same wavelength a lot. It makes it easier to do this. I know I can trust you. I know your ideas are founded in logic instead of emotion. I hope you get the same from me."

She sank back into the cushions, able to relax again now the conversation was neutral. There was no way she and Zach could hide their relationship much longer. It was going to devour her. "I do. I came up with your numbers, didn't I?"

He laughed. "That's not how I know you trust me. It's because you took the job." He worked while he talked, fingers flying over the keys even when he was looking at her. "I'm just glad you and Zach are finally getting along."

Was that a catch in his voice? Her head shot up. He stared back with the blankest expression she had ever seen. She was reading too much into his reactions. "Me too. It's nice to have the tension gone."

Silence descended over them as the conversation lulled, and they both dove back into their work. Rae was proofing a series of document templates to make sure they were error free before they went to a lawyer for review. At some point Zach rejoined them in the living room and made some notes on his laptop. The whir of fans and tapping on keyboards were the only sounds in the living room.

Zach wandered to the fridge. "Heads-up."

Scott's hand shot straight up, and a can of Mountain Dew flew across the room. He snagged it out of the air without missing a beat.

Rae snickered at the sight. Scott had been their quarterback in high school—probably the worst one the school ever had—but a person could go a long way when their father donated heavily to the team.

"What?" Scott asked. "I'm catching, not throwing. Besides, this is valuable."

"I get it. It's still funny."

Zach set a can of iced coffee on the table in front of her. When she met his gaze, something less than lighthearted stared back. The want sent a new rush through her, turning her amusement into lust. How soon could they call it a day?

This was work. Fun would wait until they were alone. Even if her thoughts were filled with memories of his hands and lips all over her bare skin. Heat flooded her. She grabbed the drink and tried to be subtle about running the icy can up the inside of her arm. It didn't help as much as she'd like.

"Are we going to make a habit of meeting here?" Scott's sudden question shattered the bubble of lust enveloping Rae's thoughts.

"It was convenient. I guess it depends," Zach replied.

The truth was Zach had spent more than half his nights there over the last week. The only way they'd managed to keep their relationship from Chloe was her sister decided they were both workaholics. Rae stared blankly at her own screen, not comprehending the words and numbers in front of her.

"How is it convenient?" Scott asked.

Why was this entire line of questioning making her paranoid?

Zach glanced at him for a second. "I was having breakfast nearby."

That was an understatement.

Scott raised an eyebrow but went back to what he was doing. Rae bit back her sigh. She was never going to forgive herself if she drove a wedge between them. When half of her asked why she hadn't thought of that before, she faltered, and it hit her. It wasn't that she was worried about being the wedge; she was terrified she'd become the third wheel. If Scott didn't take the news well, she'd be the one left out in the cold. The woman who had been stupid enough to try and find her place with them.

Fortunately, the questions died off as they each dove into their own projects. The afternoon and evening came and went, and so did the Chinese takeout.

Scott's vocal yawn bounced through the otherwise silent room. "After ten. It's been a long time since we did any work this hardcore."

Rae rubbed her eyes, trying to get some of the moisture back into them. He was right. She hadn't even realized it was so late. "It's for a good cause."

"And I completely agree." He snapped his laptop shut, unplugged the power cord, and stowed it all in his bag. "But I need sleep, or none of my estimates are going to be any good."

"He's right. Same place, same time tomorrow?" Zach mimicked his actions, packing up his computer.

Rae nodded. They were close to having the information they needed. "Another day, and we can probably make this news public."

Scott let out a short, relieved laugh. "Best thing I've heard in weeks."

They exchanged their goodbyes, and Rae locked the door behind them. She sank back into the couch. She was alone in the apartment for the first time in days. It was an odd sensation. The only sounds were from Rae's computer and the fridge.

She shook the eerie feeling away. It made sense for Zach to walk out the door with Scott, to keep up appearances, but that didn't stop her from missing him. Maybe it was time they talked about telling their friends.

Or maybe she didn't want to be the one to bring it up. Part of her was still terrified he was going to get bored with her. With them. She rubbed her eyes again. She needed a hot shower and then a good movie she'd seen a million times and could fall asleep to.

Fifteen minutes later, she emerged from the shower. She probably shouldn't be wearing one of his T-shirts over her knit shorts, but it wasn't as if anyone was going to see.

A knock startled her. Her racing heart switched gears but not speed when she answered and saw Zach standing there.

He rubbed the back of his head, his mouth crooked sheepishly. "I got halfway home and realized I forgot something."

"Oh?" His laptop had left with him. Unless he meant the clothes she was wearing. She wasn't going to think about what it meant if he wanted those back. His gaze traveled her frame from head to toe, and back again. "You wear that better than I do."

Heat flooded her cheeks, not just from his attention, but also from the images of how the shirt looked on him, just tight enough to show his wiry muscles, shifting with his every move. "That's really a matter of opinion."

"Are you busy right now?"

"Also a matter of opinion. I was thinking about watching TV and falling asleep. I have work in the morning."

"Can I kidnap you for a little while?"

She shook her head.

"Why not?"

She tangled her fingers in his. "Because I'll go willingly. Let me change first."

"You look great like you are."

"I can't go out in public like this."

"Technically where we're going isn't public." He grabbed her keys from their stand near the door, and nudged her sandals toward her. "Come on."

"Where are we going?"

"It's a surprise. Though, probably not much of one once we get close. You'll see."

Curiosity piqued, she followed him to his car, and slid into the passenger seat when he held the door open. "Do I get a hint?"

He settled in, started the engine, and pulled onto the almost empty road. "I think you'll like it."

"That's my hint?" What meant to sound like a flat retort came out with a hint of laughter. "I could have guessed that."

He pointed the car west and navigated toward the freeway. "How so?"

"I assume—maybe not rightly so, but I do anyway—that you're not going to do it if you think I won't like it."

He rested a hand on her knee, the heat from his palm sinking into her skin, soothing her. He glanced sideways at her. "No, you're right. I'd do an awful lot to see you happy."

The words warmed her more than his touch, though the combination of both sent flutters through her chest.

The conversation drifted from one random work thing to the next. How it was nice to be pulling this project together. The success they had so far. A tiny voice in the back of her head pointed out they stayed away from Scott's name and anything to do with him.

She argued with herself. It wasn't as if they were making decisions without him or keeping him out of the loop.

Except, you know, this whole hooking up with Zach thing.

They'd get around to telling him. Soon, of course. *Of course.* Great. Her own thoughts didn't believe her reasoning.

She snapped herself from the internal debate when the car slowed, and Zach pulled into an exit lane. Rae knew exactly where they were, because her parents still lived out here. Almost as far west as one could drive before hitting the mountains. They'd all grown up on this side of the valley.

Which still didn't tell her what they were doing out here. She didn't have to wait much longer. Less than five minutes later, they pulled into the student parking lot of their old high school. She still didn't understand the significance. The sight brought back a rush of powerful memories—good and bad—she thought she'd dealt with long ago. Her chest tightened, and she drew in a shaky breath.

Zach studied her. "You okay?"

Another breath and then a third, and she managed to tuck most of the potent wash of emotion away. "I'm fine."

They climbed from the car. He met her in front of the car and tangled his fingers with hers. "Come on." He tugged her toward the science building and then past it.

Her heart clenched, and another unexpected surge almost made her stumble. Their lunch tree. "What are we...?" She didn't know what she was trying to ask or why this was hitting her so hard. It was ages ago. Something she'd walked away from and never looked back. Not really, anyway.

"Sit with me." His voice was low, mingling with the quiet night instead of disrupting it. He settled with his back to the tree and tugged her down to sit between his legs, resting against his chest, the way they used to when they were younger. He draped his arms over her shoulders, and intertwined his fingers between her breasts. "Your heart is racing. Are you sure you're all right?"

She wanted to give him a coy answer. Something like *you have that effect on me*. Her mind was too much of a cluttered mess to pull out the teasing. Guilt and regret sank into her. Longing. Everything she swore to herself didn't exist when she left. "I don't know."

He traced his nose along the back of her neck, breath warm and soothing. His lips vibrated against her skin when he spoke. "Me too."

His uncertainty—a waver she wasn't used to hearing from him—mingled with her thoughts and helped calm her. At least she wasn't alone in this. She leaned more of her weight against him and covered his hands with hers.

"When we talked in my office a few weeks ago, I told you I wanted to rewrite our ending." As he spoke, his words rolled through his chest and her back.

Had it really only been a few weeks? Logically, Zach knew that was right. But in some ways it felt like a blink and in others an eternity.

"I remember," Rae said. "I don't think it worked."

He rested his forehead against her skull and inhaled her familiar scent. "That's why we're here." He wasn't sure where the inspiration had come from, but once the idea struck, he couldn't get it out of his head. "I don't want to rewrite our ending because I don't want us to end."

The tension seemed to drain from her body, and she sagged against him. "I like the sound of *us*."

He smiled even though she couldn't see it. "So, rather than closure, I think we need to catch up."

She twisted her head enough to see him, brows raised, then settled back against him again. "That's a lot to cover."

"We've got time. We'll start small." He kissed

along her shoulder and up her neck to her ear, to nip at her earlobe. "Tell me what you've been up to."

She let out a light laugh. "You know what I've been up to."

This felt so right. Her in his arms. No pretenses between them. "No. I know what you do for a living. I want details about you, not your job."

"How far back do you want to go?"

He gritted his teeth at an abrupt surge of—he wasn't sure how to describe it—everything. He pushed overwhelming sensation aside. "To the last time we were here. Well, not literally. But since…" *Everything fell apart.* The words froze in his throat. He swallowed them down. "You know."

"I do." Her voice dropped in volume, and she pulled his arms tighter. "Let's see. I, uh, had an internship offer in Chicago…"

As the past flowed between them in words, it stripped way the lingering tension. It didn't erase everything, but it lessened a sting he hadn't realized was there.

Then, as if a switch flipped, she stiffened in his arms, and her words faded into the darkness.

He nudged her. "What?"

"That's when Kelly came back, isn't it? The money. The promises."

Inky anxiety clenched in his muscles until his neck protested at the tightness. "Yup."

This time she shifted her entire frame until she faced him. "Is there more to it than that?"

Of course there was. But he wasn't sure he could explain it. There were too many mistakes on his part there. Too many assumptions. Decisions that almost destroyed everything. Mistakes. "No."

She furrowed her brows, and her smile vanished. "Of course not."

"I'm sorry. Not yet." Suddenly the closeness that had wrapped them up for the last couple of hours felt like a heavy blanket, stealing his air. "We should get home."

"Yeah. Drop me off."

He bit the inside of his cheek until it ached. That meant separate beds. Which was fair, but it didn't mean he liked it. "Of course."

chapter seventeen

Two days later, Zach trailed his fingers through Rae's hair, watching it fall back against his chest when he let go.

Her breath scurried across his skin when she sighed. Her fingers drew a line down his sternum and back up. "Morning."

"Mmm… Ditto." He moved his hand to her bare back. Neither of them had mentioned the abrupt end to the conversation at the high school the other night, and he was fine with that if it meant peace. This was the third morning this week waking up next to her, and he wondered if the novelty would ever fade. They still hadn't told anyone. Being in the same room together with Scott was tense. They stayed at Zach's place whenever Chloe was home, so her sister wouldn't ask questions, but Chloe had been at Jordan's last night. Besides, those were details to be worked out later.

Something creaked in the background, and Zach tensed. "Are you expecting visitors?"

Rae shook her head. "Probably the neighbors. They're loud sometimes."

"Lorraine." Chloe's distinct voice carried through the room.

"Shit," Rae muttered just as the bedroom door swung open. She propped herself up, holding the blanket in front of her. "Don't you knock?"

"Oh, my God." Chloe's eyes grew wide, and she

slammed the door shut again. Her call echoed through the apartment. "I did *not* need to see that."

Rae sat up, blanket falling away. "So much for keeping things quiet."

Zach traced a line down her back, up her side, and then along the curve of her breast. "Is it that big a deal? You're not ashamed of me, are you?"

She laughed. "Definitely not and don't tempt me, or I'll re-introduce you to my mother, so she believes I'm finally dating someone respectable."

The word echoed in his head. It was assumed, but neither of them had said it yet. "Are we?"

"Respectable?"

"Dating."

She looked at him, bottom lip caught between her teeth and brow furrowed. "Aren't we?"

He sat up and kissed her deeply. That hadn't lost its novelty either. "Most definitely."

She grinned and hopped out of bed. The sun spiked through sheer curtains and accented her nude silhouette for a moment before she donned a T-shirt and pair of shorts. "I'll go talk to her while you get dressed."

As soon as Rae opened the door, Chloe's voice filled the room again. "I wasn't serious when I told you to try and get me a raise by sleeping with my boss." The door drifted shut again, not entirely muffling the second part of her comment. "Did it work?"

Zach laughed and plucked his clothes off the chair Rae draped them over last night. Things had been so much easier the last few days. Making offers to people they wanted to pick up from Cord. Making plans. Doing something again. He couldn't remember why he'd ever thought it was a bad idea.

His phone vibrated on the nightstand, and as he went to answer, he noticed he'd already missed at least one call. "Yeah?"

"Are you trying to give me a heart attack?" Scott's panic was clear even over the phone.

Zach smirked. At least Scott still had something to freak out about. "Possibly. What's up?"

"You haven't listened to my messages?"

"I was sleeping." Zach pressed the speaker button and tossed the phone on the bed, talking as he dressed. "What's up?"

"It's almost ten."

Zach buttoned his shirt. "So?"

Scott's sigh filled the room. "So you haven't been served yet, have you?"

Served. Zach frowned. The single word obliterated his good mood. "What?"

"I'll take that as a no. Are you even home?"

What now? "No."

"All better." Rae burst back into the room.

Zach rubbed his face, bracing himself for the fallout.

"Rae?" Scott's question echoed through the room.

She stared at the phone on the bed, eyes wide. Her jaw moved up and down, but nothing came out.

Zach thought fast. She needed to be in on the conversation anyway. "Yeah. We ran into each other. Want to join us?"

Rae grabbed a brush off her nightstand and yanked it through her hair, then fastened each side into a simple pigtail.

"You said you were sleeping." Scott's tone had gone from panicked to flat.

"I was." Zach back pedaled. "Until an hour ago. Then I decided I wanted breakfast."

"And you just decided you didn't have to answer your phone until now?" Disbelief hung heavy in Scott's question.

"Technically, I'm between jobs. I'm trying to learn how to relax when I'm not on the clock."

Rae stepped in front of him and buttoned his shirt the rest of the way. She leaned in to whisper in his ear, "You scare me. Never lie to me like that."

He smiled, ignoring the threat behind the joke, and kissed her silently on the cheek.

"Yeah, breakfast," Scott said suddenly. "Tell me where, and I'll bring the summons, since apparently you ran out before you got yours."

Zach wracked his brain. It had to be closer to Chloe's place than Scott's, and someplace it could look like they'd been for a while.

"The bagel place on Ninth and Union," Rae said.

Zach ran the address through his head, impressed. Between them but still farther away from Scott.

"Swell. See you both in fifteen minutes." The line went dead.

Zach made sure they were disconnected before he slid his phone into his pocket. It both concerned and impressed him how easily Rae slid into his deception. "Why are we keeping this from him?"

Rae stepped away. "It's not that I think it's a big

deal. I just… It's…" She trailed off, not looking at him.

"Yeah. I know." Just because Zach understood and agreed, didn't mean it hurt any less to hear that she felt the same. He followed her into the living room. Chloe was nowhere to be seen, but her bedroom door was closed. He grabbed Rae's keys off the table by the front door and tossed them to her. "Meet you there?"

She snagged them out of the air. "Yeah."

Scott dropped a short stack of paper on the table, and the breeze ruffled napkins and bagel wrappers. He flopped onto the bench seat next to Rae with a huff.

She slid him a fresh cup of coffee. "Hazelnut."

Scott's smile looked forced. "Thanks."

Zach tried to tell himself he was relieved everything was still status quo between Rae and Scott. That their interactions were relaxed and comfortable. Exactly what they needed to be. He wasn't jealous.

"New place?" Scott asked.

Zach shrugged. "Got tired of the last one. I decided to try something new." His desire for small talk was vanishing. He grabbed the paperwork off the table. "Summons?"

Scott's scowl returned. He took a long drink. "DM has filed a cease and desist pending investigation. Say we're stealing intellectual property."

Rae made a sound that was somewhere between

a grunt and a groan. "But you're not. You're starting over. That's the point."

"No," Scott said. "The point is to tie us up in court long enough they exhaust our funds and delay our schedule."

Zach didn't argue. He knew it was true. *Fuck*, why hadn't they thought about that? Right, because they were desperate to cling to something other than despair. "Have you talked to Legal?" It was a ridiculous question. That would have been who Scott called when he couldn't get a hold of Zach. "What did he say?"

"That's what he said." Scott snatched the summons away and stuffed them into his laptop bag. "That's all he said. You had me on speaker phone in this place?"

Zach shook his head, shifting to the new topic as quickly as he could. "I was wearing my Bluetooth."

"You're trying to learn how to relax, and you had your ear piece with you?"

"Habit." Zach didn't like the direction of the questions. They needed to be planning a new strategy, not dissecting a rapidly formed cover story. "What do you mean that's all he said?"

"Technically it's not all he said." Scott studied Rae for a minute and then ignored his own drink and took a sip of her coffee. "Second cup already?"

Zach frowned. What was going on?

She blinked. "Third. I thought we might be here a while. What else did he say?"

"That he couldn't tell me anything else, and technically he'd already said too much. How did I hear her talking to you earlier? How did she hear me asking where to meet?" He looked at Zach.

"Ear piece speaker is too sensitive," Zach repeated. He was used to Scott changing the subject without pause, but he usually didn't carry on two conversations at once. "You're leaving out details. Do I need to call him myself?"

Scott pushed his drink away. "Sure. Use your ear piece, so we can all join in the conversation but no one else can."

"It's in the car." Zach wondered if he was actually going to be able to talk his way out of this one, and why he thought it mattered.

"Because…?"

Rae sighed loudly. Before Zach could reply, she said, "Because he didn't want anyone else eavesdropping. Because he's trying to learn how to not be such a workaholic. Which would you prefer?"

Scott studied her for a minute. He brushed a loose strand of hair off her forehead. "Just the truth."

Zach hid his discomfort and braced himself.

"Fine." Rae leaned back against the wall, arms crossed. "He did have you on speaker phone. I heard because he was in my bedroom. Where he's been half of the last week. We got here maybe two minutes before you did, and it's my first cup, and I haven't even had a chance to put cream and sweetener in it. Which you were kind enough not to call me on."

Scott rubbed his eyes before looking at her again. "So you're fucking him."

She cringed and turned away from his glare.

Scott slammed his fist on the table, making all the cups—and Rae—jump. "You're smarter than that. Why would you go after him?"

Zach glared at him. Was that really the opinion Scott held of him? Hypocritical much?

Rae clenched her jaw. "I'm smart enough to not let you dictate who I do and don't pursue. I've got much better taste."

"I knew you liked him." Something unfamiliar flashed in Scott's eyes.

Malice. Zach's gut sank.

"I didn't think he cared about you." Scott focused on Rae again. "You're not his type. You'd need to be about six inches taller and ten pounds lighter."

Fury raced through Zach, and he was on his feet in a second, yanking Scott up by the T-shirt. "You don't get to take this out on her because you're jealous. You know none of that is true."

Scott's eyes narrowed, his hands balling into fists. He planted his feet shoulder width apart. "I don't really know much of anything right now. I mean, I thought I was just being paranoid wondering if my best friends were fucking each other behind my back."

Rae scrambled to stand and wedged her way between them. Her hand covered Zach's, and she nudged him back. "What did your attorney say?" Her words filtered through clenched teeth.

Scott didn't look at her, still glaring at Zach. "Nothing significant. Just that we're about to be held up in court indefinitely, wasting away our savings when we could be on an island somewhere instead."

Rae planted a hand on each of their chests and shoved them farther apart. Her palms were hot, and a tremor ran through her arm.

How was Zach going to get her out of the way? "You were the one who didn't want to give up." He didn't want to be having this argument here, but he wasn't going to walk away. This wasn't the standard bullshit they'd been through since the takeover. His blood roared with an unfamiliar rage. "You blew a fuse when I even mentioned retirement. Accused me of abandoning a dream. You latched onto her idea the moment she brought it up, and you should have. It's a fantastic fucking idea."

Scott didn't defend himself. "Did I mention our lawyer is bailing on us because his firm is being retained by the company who's suing us? Maybe someone who was doing the paperwork might have caught that?" He glared at Rae.

"No." Zach put as much emphasis on the word as he could. He rested a hand on Rae's arm and gently tugged her out of the way. "Don't take this out on her. She spent a few days with our records. We've had them for years. I could have seen it coming better than her. Or maybe you might have noticed it."

"Holy fuck, stop defending her. This is what we pay her for. Or maybe that's just an excuse to keep your piece of tail on payroll?" Scott glared at Rae. "Is that how you got him to go along with this?"

Zach wasn't thinking anymore, and he was only vaguely aware of his own fist pulling back. It never got a chance to connect.

Rae punched Scott in the arm, the smack echoing through the entire shop. "Move." The threat in her voice was distinct.

"I didn't mean it." The corners of Scott's mouth

pulled down.

"Get the fuck out of my way right now." Steel lined her command. "Or I'll move you and grind your balls into the tile in the process."

Scott stepped aside. "I'm sorry."

"You're not." She shouldered past him. "You wouldn't have said it if you didn't mean it. You're acting like a spoiled child. I think you've got more of your father in you than you like to admit."

Zach smirked joylessly at the insult. It would hurt more than any fist, though he was still considering throwing a punch.

Scott's shoulders slumped. "Please?"

She held up a hand. "Don't. I did all of this for you."

"You slept with my best friend for me?"

She stepped closer to him until they were toe-to-toe then looked up at him. "Tell you what. I have a solution for you. There's enough money in your budget for another employee since you're not renting office space. I hear your CFO is resigning. Maybe look into using it to hire an attorney—and consider yourself lucky said individual isn't adding to the stack of lawsuits with sexual harassment."

Zach processed the words. She couldn't quit. She hadn't even started yet.

"No, Rae..." Scott started, but nothing else came out.

"Don't worry about it." The emotion was gone from her voice. "Zach was right. I'm just going to fuck everything up. You've got your numbers. You've used me for everything you needed to. Go get successful again. I'll leave you both alone."

Had he just been dumped? Zach grabbed her wrist before she could walk away. "Wait."

She directed her glare at him.

Zach let go. He should go after her, but he didn't know if he could find the right things to say. He directed every ounce of fury and anger he could at Scott. For the first time in he didn't know how long, he couldn't find a single word for the flames raging inside.

chapter eighteen

Rae sat at her desk—correction, the desk in her sister's guest bedroom. It had been three days since she walked out on Zach and Scott in the coffee shop. It was childish, but she'd ignored all their messages and calls. Scott's words still echoed in her head every time she let her thoughts wander.

You're not his type. You'd need to be about six inches taller and ten pounds lighter.

The venom crawled through her veins until every inch of her ached. This was only supposed to be an extended vacation. A chance to hang out with her sister while Rae looked for a new job. A break from life.

I thought I was just being paranoid wondering if my best friends were fucking each other behind my back.

The accusation bounced in her skull. She rubbed her eyes and tried to force the memory away. Why had she tried to turn it into more? Sure, the time spent with Zach was incredible. God, it couldn't have been anything but and still hurt this much. It was still borrowed. All of this. She'd known that from the start, and ignored it.

Is this just an excuse to keep your piece of tail on the payroll?

No. It meant more than that. Her idea wasn't a way to keep herself in Zach's life. This was for the people she cared about, right?

Or was she really so selfish she'd talked them into an idea without thinking it through just to get back a life she surrendered years ago?

A knock echoed through the apartment—someone at the front door—and Rae dropped her head in her arms. She couldn't ignore this forever. She needed to talk to Zach, at least. She owed him that.

She wasn't so sure about Scott.

You're not his type...You'd need to be—

Chloe's loud whoop cut through painful thoughts, and Rae redirected her focus to outside her head.

She shook the haunting voice aside. This wasn't doing her any good. She grabbed her phone and dialed.

"Rae?" Zach's voice was distorted by background noise. "Hey."

Ambivalence warred inside. Joy and sadness. "Where are you?"

"The airport. I'm glad you called. Silly question, but how soon can you be here?"

"Where are you going?" Was he making good on his promise to pack it all in and buy a one-way ticket to Europe? *Shit.*

"Chicago. You didn't listen to my voice mails. I have a lead on some inexpensive development hardware, and I need to take a look in person. Come with me."

He was still moving ahead with business as normal. Relief and joy filled her at the realization, but something bitter tempered it. They could do this without her. *Of course they can.*

"I can't." She wasn't sure how this situation was going to work itself out, but she knew if she went with him, it would make things worse. "It won't solve anything."

"Then fuck this entire idea. Meet me here, and we'll figure out a new plan."

"You'd never forgive yourself if you blew this off."

His sigh amplified the noise around him. "I won't be doing any better if I blow you off."

It was selfish of her to smile, but she couldn't help it. "Take your trip. We'll talk when you get back."

"Promise me."

Something whispered in her head, asking if she could keep that promise. "Of course."

"Rae?"

"Hmm?"

"Nothing." The word was clipped. "Talk to you soon."

"Yeah." She disconnected and dropped her phone on the desk. That had gone about as middle-of-the-road as was possible. She rubbed her face. *Now what?*

"Lorraine!" Chloe's shout was accompanied by a pounding on the bedroom door.

Find out why her sister was screaming loud enough for everyone in every surrounding apartment to hear. "What?"

The door creaked open. "I got my offer." Chloe all but skipped across the room, and threw her arms around Rae's neck. "You made it work."

Rae hugged her back. "I just had an idea. They made it work."

"Whatever." Chloe pulled back and looked her in the eye. "What kind of magic tricks do you have to get Jordan out of his Cord contract?"

He was one of the few who survived staff cuts, and he'd had to make a difficult choice. Staying with Cord and DM meant his name would be smeared all over their upcoming game. But it also meant working with a group of people he didn't care for. Leaving meant the job he wanted, but he'd have to wait a year before signing with Scott and Zach, because of the non-compete clause he'd signed when Cord hired him. The clause that was only erased with the severance offers.

Rae saw both sides of the argument and knew it had been tough on him to decide. "Contracts aren't really my specialty." Understatement of the decade, apparently. The argument from the other morning tried to force its way back, and she shelved it.

"Talk to him," Chloe said.

"Jordan?"

Chloe raised her brows, and pursed her lips. "Scott. You're not doing anyone any good sitting in here and moping. Or at least go buy us some ice cream, so you can mope and I can celebrate."

Rae rolled her eyes, but smiled. "Why should I call him?"

"He's your best friend."

She hadn't told Chloe the details of their argument the other day and saw no reason to. Her sister deserved this job, and Rae didn't want to taint her opinion. "I'm pretty sure he'll be okay without me."

Chloe glanced behind her then turned her gaze to her feet. "Bullshit."

"Excuse me?"

"Ignore for a minute that he's my boss and gave me this chance, and it's the best job I ever had. None of that matters right now." Chloe shifted her weight, still studying her shoes. "He's been there, by your side, since I was little. The two of you need each other."

It was a sweet sentiment made bitter by the situation. "Did you ever think he and I would…end up together?" Rae had no idea where the question came from.

Chloe's head shot up, and the look in her wide eyes said she was wondering the same thing. "God, no."

"Why not?" Rae knew her own reasons, but now she was curious. Her stomach dropped into her feet when Scott stepped into the doorway behind Chloe, face an impassive mask.

Chloe couldn't have seen him the way she stood, but she also had to know he was in the apartment. "It's hard to explain. I just… You two don't challenge each other. It's too easy for you to settle when you're together. Which is great for unwinding, but horrible for things like personal growth."

Rae refused to look at him. "I don't think we're

quite that compatible. A few days I would have agreed, so I can see why you'd say that, but it's not true."

"At least let me apologize," Scott hovered in the doorway.

"No." Rae was on her feet, irritation coursing through her. Her sister had set her up. Chloe tended to do things like that, but this was different.

"Stop." Chloe grabbed her arm, spinning her so they were toe-to-toe and stared her down. "Hear him out."

"You don't know what he said to me."

"I do. He told me. You also kept something really big from him." Chloe let go of her and stepped out of the way. "I'm not taking sides. You both suck in the friends department as far as I'm concerned. But I told him I'd ask you, and now I have."

Scott moved into the room but still kept his distance. "It hurt that neither of you told me what was going on. I saw it and told myself you wouldn't keep that from me."

Rae didn't want to hear this. She stalked toward the door, coming up short when he blocked her path.

"Never tell anyone you heard me admit this, but I was wrong," he said. "It doesn't matter what you did or didn't do. I was wrong to say those things. I was hurt, I knew it would hurt in return, and I shouldn't have done it."

She pushed him, but not hard enough to knock him out of the way. "Don't steal my thunder like that, you asshole."

"So are we talking again?"

"No." She didn't know how long it would take

to get over the sting of his insults, but she also knew it wasn't him. "And you're not forgiven."

"That's fair. Let me buy you coffee."

"Bribery won't change anything."

"There's a place just a few blocks away." He nodded toward the street.

"I know it." She grabbed her purse and shoes. "You owe me big."

As the door swung shut behind them, Chloe called, "Stay out as long as you need."

"I owe you so very much more than just an *I'm sorry*." Scott kept pace with her as they headed toward the street. "Walk?"

She nodded. They'd probably get there faster. Rae needed to hang onto some of her anger, but she also hated the idea of being mad at Scott. She didn't know what else to do for now besides let him talk.

"I've always wanted this," he said. "When I thought we'd lost it, I was lost." He glanced at her. "I can't thank you enough for helping me—both of us—keep it. You were right. I can't do this without Zach."

The words drilled into her already jumbled thoughts. At least they agreed on that. The thing was, now that she'd done her part, she was more certain than ever they could do it without her. It wasn't a derogatory thought. She specialized in helping companies find their financial footing and then moved on.

That didn't make the realization they'd be fine without her, at least company-wise, hurt any less. And this company was everything to them.

chapter nineteen

Rae tried to blink away the sting behind her eyelids. She swallowed, and her raw throat protested. She didn't want to be doing this, but there was no choice. She swore to herself she would do this professionally, and that meant offering her resignation officially and in person. Besides, she knew if she didn't say goodbye, it would devour her.

She knocked on Zach's familiar door. At least her time here had been nice. She avoided his calls when he landed last night, wanting to talk face to face, and at the same time, terrified. It was the right decision though. She clutched her briefcase in front of her. She didn't need it, but it gave her something to cling to and fiddle with.

Zach opened the front door, his surprise morphing into a soft smile. "Hey."

She made sure her expression didn't give anything away. "Good morning. I hope this is a good time."

He reached for her and then stopped. "Something's wrong."

It looked like he wanted to say more. She was glad he didn't.

"Come in." He nodded toward the living room.

"Thank you, but no. I won't be here long." She winced inwardly at her own formal tone, but it was better this way. She just had to keep telling herself that.

"I missed—You look good."

That hadn't been her intention. The below-the-knee skirt and suit jacket were supposed to say *all business*, not earn her compliments. She retrieved an envelope from the pocket of her briefcase. "I thought I'd make this official."

Zach grabbed it and started to tear it in half.

The gesture dug deep, gnawing at raw wounds. She smiled and shook her head. "That won't change anything."

"You can't. We can't do it without you."

"Yeah, you can." She ignored the ache throbbing behind her ribcage. "You just can't do it without each other. Besides, I'm leaving."

"Just like that?"

"Not just like that. I accepted the offer I had before..." She couldn't finish the thought. Before what? Before they kept such a big secret from someone so important? Before she surrendered her heart even though she knew better? "Something came in that lets me get paid and keeps you all in business as well."

"Where are you going?"

"Washington. The offer isn't as good as something like CFO, but it's enough to make it worth my time." Her resignation and leaving meant something else, too. She hadn't officially broken it off with him, but the entire conversation implied it.

"What about us?" The emotion vanished from his voice, and the question was flat.

She knew the answer. She just had to tell him. It was the thought that haunted her more than any other. She'd left him once to keep his plans for the future from impacting her career, and she'd been mistaken. Things weren't so cloudy this time though. Lust wasn't a good excuse for breaking up the potential their business held… All she had to do was say so, but the words wouldn't form. "What do you think?"

He lifted her chin, forcing her to look him in the eye. "You have to say it."

"There's no us."

"So you're going to do it again." He dropped his hand, disdain echoing in his statement.

She deserved the irritation directed at her. "Not quite. No spending years blaming you for something that's not your fault." She forced out the last two words. "No regrets."

She stepped back. She needed to leave soon because her composure wouldn't hold much longer. "The two of you need each other. Not in the you're-an-adorable-couple kind of way your developers joke about, but you work too well together. I can't be what comes between you. And honestly, I can't take being the verbal punching bag for your testosterone-fueled arguments anymore. Goodbye. Good luck."

Zach stepped up next to her and cupped the back of her neck with one hand.

A moan pulsed in her raw throat, and she swallowed it. Her expression never shifted.

He kissed her softly.

Desire screamed through her, and she beat it back. It took the last of her self-control not to return the gesture. She kept her mouth still and eyes open, staring at him blankly until he pulled away.

He frowned.

She turned away before the tears started leaking from her eyes and walked out the front door.

"Rae." Zach's voice froze her feet to the ground.

She couldn't turn around. Facing him again would hurt too much, and her grip on her composure was almost gone. "What?"

"You're really doing this."

She tried to keep her response steady. "I have to."

"You don't." The two words were heavy. "Scott will get over whatever his issue is. If you really think it's best, you don't have to work for us. Don't go."

Why couldn't he just let her leave? Her resolve weakened every moment she stood there. She blinked back the tears, and faced him. "It's not just about Scott. Or who is or isn't working with you." Each word was more painful than the last.

His blue eyes were clouded with hurt. "Then explain it to me."

She threw up her hands, as frustrated with her lack of words as with his persistence. "It's everything. I'm already a part of it, and if I stay, that won't change. I'll get sucked in again, because that's what happens."

She was unable to stop the words flowing from her. "And then we'll break up. It'll suck. It'll devour at least one of us. Worse than it is now. And even though stuff like that happens all the time, it usually doesn't involve multimillion-dollar companies. You don't want another Kelly, and even though I don't plan on screwing anyone over, we're already proving none of us is mature enough to keep our personal lives and work separate."

His brow knit together. "What makes you so sure you and I are doomed?"

"Really?" She couldn't keep the disbelief from her voice. "We couldn't even tell people we were dating. You still keep yourself closed off. We can be baring our souls, and you'll just randomly hold something back. That doesn't bode well for our future together."

He stared back, lips drawn in a tight line, not moving or speaking. The seconds ticked away.

Did he expect her to say something? She'd pretty much spewed it all. She wasn't going to babble just to fill the air.

Finally he shook his head. "Got it. Have a nice life." He turned away, marched back to the house, and then yanked open the front door.

It slammed shut behind him, glass rattling in the frame. Rae forced herself to make it to her car and then leave the driveway, before she started sobbing. When she was out of view of the house, she pulled over and let the tears have their way. She shook as grief and regret pounded over her.

chapter twenty

"Your next appointment is waiting for you."

Rae smiled at her assistant, Alice. Odd that the potential client wasn't in the waiting room. Maybe whoever it was had wanted some privacy for a phone call or something. "Thanks. Who am I seeing?"

Alice checked her computer. "Rinslet Enterprises. They're looking for distribution channels."

The name tickled something in the back of her mind, but she couldn't grasp it. The appointment was status quo. "Do we have lunch reservations anywhere?"

Alice blushed. "I'll get you something."

That was a strange reaction. "Thanks."

Rae stepped into her office, letting the door swing shut behind her when she saw her guest. Her feet stuck to the floor. *It can't be.*

Zach stood and straightened his suit coat, looking very much the part of a business man. He offered his hand.

She shook it, pasting a cool smile into place. Her heart hammered so hard in her chest, she thought it might escape. What was he doing there? "Mister Johnston."

His mouth twisted, but he sat when she took her place across the desk from him. He couldn't be there. It wasn't fair. How had he even found her? She was going to kill Chloe if her sister had given up the information. It had taken her months to convince herself leaving was the right thing to do, and countless one-night stands—or one failed ones—to figure out she couldn't do casual sex anymore. She had finally started to move on. "What can I do for you?"

"Rae." His tone didn't give anything away.

Hearing her say her name dug deep. She wouldn't let it hurt. It didn't matter. She didn't miss him so much it haunted her every day. "Lorraine," she said. "Ms. Nielson, if you'd prefer."

"First names are fine." His cool tone matched hers. "As I'm sure Alice told you, my company is looking for a business partner."

Something leapt in Rae's chest, and she bit it back. That meant they really did need distribution channels. So they were doing well? She felt a spark of joy, but didn't dwell on it. "Usually someone in sales handles these meetings, but let me tell you what we can do for you." She opened a drawer and grabbed a marketing packet.

"I'm familiar with your business, thank you." He leaned forward, resting his forearms on her desk. "I have a proposal, if you've got time."

There was something in his words she couldn't pin down. Something in the way he phrased his statements was intentionally misleading. Might as well find out sooner rather than later. She could land the account, assign it to someone to manage, and start to try and forget his existence again. "You're on my calendar. I have time."

"Perfect." He smiled, a hint of something less formal leaking into it. He reached across her desk and hit a speed dial button on her phone.

Her curiosity and discomfort grew.

"Yeah?" Alice's voice filled the room.

"Alice, hon." His tone was smooth. "Are we set?"

"Yes, sir. They're expecting you in twenty minutes."

"Thanks. You're a doll."

She giggled, and the line went dead.

She glared at him. "You flirted with my assistant?"

He smirked. "Someone had to tell me where your favorite place was around here. Chloe sure as hell won't talk about you."

"And you were arrogant enough to assume I'd hear you out." She desperately wanted to be furious, but the situation was both flattering and amusing. She should throw him out right then. Kick his ass to the curb and pretend he'd never been there. "Do you even actually want to talk about distribution?"

Zach nodded. "I told you I had a proposal. Didn't have to make any of that up."

It didn't escape her he technically didn't answer the question. Her curiosity was gnawing at her now. She grabbed her purse. "I guess we should get going then."

He stood when she did. The strange mixture of

a standard business meeting combined with the familiarity of the way he spoke and held himself added to her uneasy tension. He fell into step beside her as they made their way to the elevator, his arm inches from hers but never making contact.

I won't lose it in the middle of the office. I definitely won't demand he explain himself in front of everyone I work with. The two phrases repeated in her head.

She kept her teeth clenched as they got in the elevator, not sure if she was relieved or disappointed it was empty.

"So, how have you been?" he asked.

"Fantastic." She cringed when she realized there was too much enthusiasm in her reply. Might as well roll with it. "Never better. You?"

"Same." His posture was relaxed except for drumming his fingers on his leg.

Damn it. He was being infuriating. The corners of his mouth still pulled up, laughter dancing in his eyes.

They stepped into the parking garage, and she clicked the locks and alarm off on her car.

Zach grabbed her keys. "I'll drive. You navigate."

"But..." She couldn't even form a rational protest.

He held the front passenger door open for her. "Nice ride."

"Thanks." She slid into the seat. "It came with the job." His every move was too well orchestrated, and she hated it. Even more, she hated the part of her enjoying the mystery and attention.

♥ ♥ ♥

Rae drummed her fingernails on the menu, telling herself for the millionth time she couldn't order wine in the middle of the work day. Or anything stronger. The entire ride, every time she tried to find out what was going on, Zach changed the subject. He kept up a smattering of the most random small talk she'd ever heard, asking her about her apartment, her job, where her favorite coffee place was.

And she'd fallen into all of it, momentarily losing herself in the easy banter rather than thinking about the big picture. Her behavior was as infuriating as his.

After the waiter took their orders, Zach held up a manila folder. "It's driving you nuts, isn't it?"

She resisted the urge to snatch it out of his hands. "You're not endearing yourself to me, if that's what you're asking." Except despite the words, the longer they chatted, the more she was glad to see him. *Damn it.* It was going to hurt to send him away again.

For a moment his smile looked genuine. He handed her the folder.

She took it and gave him a suspicious glare before setting it on the table in front of her. She opened it cautiously, almost expecting something to jump out at her. Instead, a simple letterhead sat inside. A single sheet of paper with a logo stenciled in silver across the top.

"Rinslet Enterprises," she said aloud. That was why the name sounded familiar. It was an old memory. Back in high school when Scott first started talking about starting his own software company, it was the name she had suggested he use. The memory added to the dull ache inside.

She scanned the letter with her name at the top. Her eyes grew wide, and she read it again. It was too familiar. She'd seen it before. Except a year ago, the job offer hadn't had the new logo on it, and there had been a salary attached to it. This time it just said *to be negotiated.*

"Well?" Zach asked.

"You're joking."

"Kind of a costly way to get a laugh at your expense, don't you think? I told you I had a proposal."

No. She refused to accept it. It beat back the screaming part of her that wanted to say yes. "This isn't a proposal. It's a job offer."

"Now you're just trying to tie me up on a technicality." His mask slipped, worry creasing his brow. It was gone again as soon as it had appeared.

She beat back the desire to fall into comfortable conversation. He wanted business, she could do all business. "So, tell me how things are going with the company. Where it's at, what you've been up to. What your plans are for the future?"

"Chloe hasn't told you any of that?"

"Chloe and I don't talk about work."

Lunch came and went, and Rae continued to ask as many random questions as she could think of. They had taken her advice to hire a lawyer. He'd helped them find the loopholes they needed to continue development until the intellectual property legal battle was over. Now that it was out of the way, they were getting ready to announce their upcoming game at E3.

The check arrived, and Zach grabbed it away before she could. "So, that's my spiel. What do you think?"

She hated the part of herself objecting to what she was about to say, but it needed to be done. The fact that he still had this impact on her—that her guard was dropping even as she tried to keep him at a distance—was proof her reasons for leaving a year ago were still valid. Even if he had gone out of his way to find her. Even though it was amazing to see him again, regardless of the formal walls. "It sounds like you're doing fantastic. I'm flattered, really, but I'm going to have to say no."

His smug smile slipped away, eyes softening, and a pleading edge leaked into his voice. "You're the only person who knows how to do this. Things are falling apart without you. We need your mind and ideas."

He didn't want her back in his life because of what they had been. That was only fair, right? She hadn't been any nicer to him. It hurt, no matter how she tried to spin it in her head. "There are a lot of other people who can do what I do. Some of them probably even live closer than three states away."

His face hardened again. He stood and shook her hand. "I understand. Thank you for your time."

"Of course." She ignored the sparks flowing between them and let go as soon as was polite. "Do you need a ride back to your hotel or the airport?"

"No, thank you. I'll call a cab."

"Pleasure meeting with you, then." Rae swallowed the bile rising in her throat. This was the right thing. It was. It was. *It was.*

Wasn't it?

She stood, and focused on keeping her gait steady as she strode toward the front door. Why wouldn't the hollow ache in her chest go away?

chapter twenty-one

Rae grabbed a pint of ice cream from the freezer. She stared at it for a moment before deciding brownie chunks and chocolate chip cookie dough would only make her more ill, and she put it away again. How long would it take to get over him this time? To convince herself she made her decision because it was in everyone's best interests?

The doorbell rang, and she jumped in surprise. Who the hell was visiting her? She hadn't exactly been social or picked up any friends over the past year.

Her stomach flopped when she saw Zach through the peephole. Despite the voice screaming in her head to pretend she wasn't home, she opened the door.

He looked her over, one eyebrow raised. "Did I wake you?"

She glanced down, flushing when she remembered she was already in pajama bottoms and a T-shirt. "No. This is just around-the-house stuff. If Alice gave you my home address, she's fired."

His confident smile was gone, replaced with something more genuine. There was an upturn to his eyes, and his cheeks didn't look frozen in place. "No. I... Um... Chloe gave it to me."

"Glad to know she can be trusted with my private information." She wanted to be furious with her sister, but a spreading warmth inside wouldn't let her. "Come on in." She should tell him to leave. The desire wasn't there.

"I talked to Scott after lunch." His casual tone wavered. "He said to tell you he misses you terribly."

It was a nice thing to hear, but it wasn't quite what she needed. She talked to Scott every couple of days, and he wasn't who she missed. Besides, he kept this from her. Probably served her right. She wandered into the kitchen, instinct driving her to be a polite hostess. At least, she tried to convince herself it wasn't because she cared if he was comfortable. "Just him?"

"Nice place." His voice stayed close. "And I'm not answering that yet."

She shrugged, grabbed a can of Mountain Dew out of the fridge, and then set it on the island that separated the living room from the kitchen. She snagged a Diet Coke for herself. "Why are you here?" she asked.

He slid onto a barstool. "Not to fight. I know we've mastered that, but I was hoping we could talk."

She took a swallow of her drink. She wasn't going to enjoy this conversation. Not at all. Something else must explain the heat flooding her, making it difficult to think, right? "I'm listening. You can start any time."

"Not quite what I had in mind." He pulled a

lighter from his pocket and twirled it on the Formica counter. "I was hoping we could be pleasant instead of defensive."

Of course he was. That was the way all business transactions worked, right? "Kind of like this afternoon? Flustering and confounding me until I was almost ready to beg for answers?"

"You wanted all business, I kept it all business." He pulled his gaze away. "But I am sorry. It sounded clever in my head to try and catch you off guard, but I shouldn't have done it."

She sighed and leaned back against the counter. What did he want her to do? "I'm having a hard time keeping up. Maybe you could feed me my lines, and this would be easier."

"Yeah, I guess it would be, wouldn't it?" His fingers drummed against the side of his drink, a hollow clink echoing through the room. "How about this? I'm getting really tired of you deciding you can just walk out of my life."

Great, now he was casting blame. She crossed her arms. "So sorry to inconvenience you."

"But…" He held up his hand. "I suspect you're just as unhappy with me treating parts of our personal lives like an ongoing negotiation."

"Maybe."

"So, tell me why you actually left a year ago."

She unhooked her arms, rested her palms on the counter, and then pushed herself up to sit on it. Her feet kicked back and forth. The words weren't there. Nothing seemed appropriate. "I can't."

"I'll tell you why I'm really here instead." His voice sounded strained. "After you left, things fell apart. I mean, really bad. Scott was sporting a black eye for a week."

"Wait, what?" She hadn't expected that. No one had told her about that.

Zach gave her a sheepish smile. "He's big, but I'm fast. I was furious about what he said to you."

"He did apologize for that." Rae didn't know if she was more disturbed, flattered, or amused by the imagery. She liked the chivalry more than she wanted to admit.

"I know, but I was still pissed." He traced circles around his can top. "About everything. It took Scott months to convince me we needed you back."

The information hurt, but she knew she deserved it. "What changed your mind?"

"I told you, everything fell apart." He dropped his chin into the palm of one hand. "Everything I said at lunch was true. I just left out a couple tiny details."

So he really didn't want her back because he missed her. She shouldn't be hurt. It was what she was pretending she wanted to hear. "What kind of details?"

He paused for a few moments. "The thing is… We've eaten through our distribution and advertising budgets. I blew the last of it on E3."

She couldn't keep the skepticism off her face.

"I couldn't help it. It's our big chance to get everything back."

"We had this conversation at lunch. There are a lot of people out there who could do the job. I'm not the only one."

"Yeah, you are."

"I have a hard time believing that." She jumped

from the counter.

"And we miss you." He twisted the pop top on his can until it came off. He rolled it between his fingers, eyes never leaving the aluminum trinket. "*I miss you.*"

She kept quiet, trying to ignore her hammering heart. The words she was desperate to hear, even if she wouldn't let herself admit it.

He never looked up. "It works in my favor that I love the woman who can save our company, but I wouldn't be asking you to do this if I doubted your skill."

Love? She didn't want to hear that. Even though her heart soared and her stomach fluttered at the confession hidden in his words.

"I don't have any delusions about you jumping into my arms and returning the sentiment." He gave a bitter laugh. "But since I asked for honesty, I figured you deserve the same."

She hated the hope and the need and the desire that all wanted to hold onto what he was saying. "If I come back, it will be because I believe in what you're doing, not because I see a future with…" She couldn't finish the sentence the way she wanted to. "Anyone."

Zach frowned. "I can accept that. It'll hurt, but at least we'll get to keep Rinslet."

"How do I know—" She ducked her head, measuring her words carefully. "How do you know any of this is a good idea? What makes you think I can fix it? What makes you think you lo—" She choked on the word. "Have feelings for me?"

He shrugged. "Neither one is certain, but you

made the figures work last time, so I have faith you can do it again. As for you and me… There's a spark, right? It's not just physical. You make me think, you drag a passion out of me I try hard to hide, and I enjoy your company. You're not like anyone I've ever met, including the little girl you were back in the day."

She didn't know how to respond. Part of her understood exactly what he was saying. Deep down, she felt the same way about him, but she struggled with how much of her reaction was genuine and how much was clinging to what she wanted to hear. She gave him the only answer she could think of. "I'll take a look at your books again. I don't promise anything, and I won't take the job if I can't help, but I'll see what I can do."

"How long will it take?" He produced a USB stick from his pocket and set it next to his lighter.

"I, um…" She hadn't meant right then, but she didn't want to tell him no. Something inside her wanted him to stick around a little longer. "It depends on how much has changed. An hour to take it all in, at least."

"I'm in town at least until tomorrow afternoon. I know you have work, but is there any way…?"

She grabbed the USB drive off the counter, and flipped it back and forth between her fingers. "What are you doing tonight?"

Zach gave her a half smile. "Going back to my hotel. Seeing what's on HBO."

She couldn't believe she was about to do this, but it felt more right than any decision she'd made in a long time. "Do you want to hang out here? I've got HBO."

♥♥♥

Rae's face scrunched up, and she blinked, trying to get some moisture back in her eyes. The glow from the computer screen exaggerated the shadows in the dim kitchen. It didn't matter how many times she rearranged the numbers—the money wasn't there.

She leaned back in the chair and stretched, her T-shirt creeping up her stomach. She straightened it out when she sat up again. An hour had become four. Stubbornness wouldn't let her give up, but it wasn't giving her the answers either.

Zach had hovered when she started, but she made him go sit down. It didn't keep him from glancing in her direction every few minutes.

He gave her a weak smile and crossed the room to her fridge. A second glow whispered through the darkness when he opened the door, illuminating his wrinkled shirt.

She studied the way his arms and back moved under the fabric, but looked away before the memories could resurface. Part of the delay in her work was because she kept replaying his words over and over in her head. She was starting to believe she felt the same way, and it terrified her. All the reasons she left a year ago rushed back in the jumble of fear. What if they didn't work out? What if that destroyed this thing they'd built and then rebuilt?

And what if none of that happens, and it's as amazing as I hope?

He crossed the room and set a can on the table. "How does it look?"

She tried to ignore the tingle when his hand

brushed her arm and the twinge of disappointment when he stepped back. She took a long swallow of the cold coffee drink. "Same as last time you asked. And the time before. And always. It looks like two rich kids who don't understand the concept of restricted spending have blown through your advertising budget six months faster than they should have."

"Yeah, that sounds about right." He leaned over her, chest brushing her shoulder. "Those are the numbers?"

She nodded, glum spreading through her. She'd been through every option she could think of. Pre-orders wouldn't help the way she projected originally, since they couldn't afford their own distribution and retailers wouldn't pay out until release day. They didn't even have enough left for a basic cable ad. Well, maybe one, but not if they wanted to do anything else. "Look at it this way. If one of you mortgages your house, you should be able to pay for some pay-per-click ads and maybe a couple of gaming magazine spots."

"Really?" His voice was teasing. "Scott's definitely since mine is home base."

She giggled. "Nice."

"I've missed your laugh."

A pulse of want raced over her, and she pushed away from him, almost toppling her chair. She hoped the heat flooding her face didn't show. The conflict inside gnawed at her exhaustion. "Don't."

He frowned. "So I'm really the only one this is killing."

Regret and longing filled her. "I… I'm sorry."

He crossed his arms, expression hardening. "Just make the numbers work. That's what I'm supposed to say now, right?"

When he turned away, emptiness throbbed inside her. She licked her lips, mouth suddenly dry. "Wait."

"What?" He didn't turn around.

The chair's metal casters screeched on the tile when she stood. She closed the distance between them but didn't dare touch him. "I didn't… I just— I'm sorry."

He shrugged, muscle rippling under skin along his back. "We'll find the money somewhere."

Her pain grew at the callous response. "Not about that."

He whirled back to face her. "I can't do this. You push me away, you want me back, you lean closer, you pull away. I mean it when I say it's devouring me."

She swallowed and stepped forward. Resting a hand on his chest, she felt his heartbeat racing against her palm. He was as nervous as she was. "Do you want to know why I left?"

"You missed your cue. That was your line five hours ago."

She didn't look away. It ached to look him in the eye, but she had to let him know she was being sincere. "I was terrified of how intense this is. Something this hot and passionate burns out." As the words spilled out, their truth sank deep. Why had she never realized that before? "We can't afford to burn out. This is more than just how we feel about each other. You don't want Kelly to happen again, and I don't either. But even now, I feel empty without you."

His gaze raked over her face. "Just because the fire shifts, doesn't mean it has to fade or go out. Cord was a huge risk. We blew everything on it, and in the end, we almost lost it all. Rinslet, that's like doubling down on zero at the roulette table after winning the first time. It's worth the risk though. I'd never forgive myself if I walked away. Neither would Scott."

He traced a thumb over her cheek, and cupped her neck. "I feel the same way about you and me. Except with us, I don't see the same risk. Still, I'd never let myself live it down if I walked away from you without trying. It destroys me every time you leave, and that's part of how I know it's real."

She didn't want to hear that because she knew exactly what he meant. Acknowledging it meant admitting she didn't feel complete without him. "Having you here now is incredible, even if we're just working, but..."

He put a finger on her lips. "I'm running out of words to tell you how much I want you, but it's more important to me you're happy. I honestly think you and I can make it work, but only if you're interested."

"Maybe." She was more than interested, but it couldn't be as simple as he made it sound.

"You have to be at least a little more certain than that." He wrapped his fingers around hers and tugged her toward the bedroom. "You're not listening. I'll show you what I mean, instead."

She followed him, curious. "Show me...?"

He paused just inside the bedroom door. "You

worked really hard tonight." He moved behind her, hands on her arms, chest against her back. "And even if we don't have an answer, we'll find one."

She smiled at the tender words. She adored this side of him no one ever got to see. "I can take a little more hard, if that's what you've got in mind."

He chuckled. "Don't move."

"Why?" Air rushed in around her as he let go.

She assumed he'd stepped away, she just couldn't tell how far. A moment later, his hands rested on her shoulders. "Let me spoil you for the night."

His request was pleading mixed with command, and she couldn't refuse the combination. She nodded.

His thumbs kneaded into her neck, and she sighed. That felt incredible.

"You're too tense." He massaged deeper. "This might need some more serious attention." His hands dropped to her hips. "May I?"

She wasn't sure exactly what he was asking, but as long as it involved feeling more of him, she was game. "Yes."

He stripped off her shirt and tossed it aside. The air conditioner cooled her skin, and her nipples hardened. His fingers glided along her spine, and he unhooked her bra, letting it fall away.

Anticipation raced through her, slick wetness pooling between her legs. He hooked his thumbs in the elastic of her bottoms and shoved the rest of her clothing to the floor, never touching her with more than his hands.

His whisper caressed the outer edge of her ear.

"Lie on the bed on your stomach."

"Okay." She did as she was told. What was he up to? The cool cotton soothed but didn't erase the heat flooding her bare skin.

A moment later, a new weight rested against the back of her legs, and his skin met the outside of her thighs. She turned her head enough to see him straddling her, wearing nothing but his boxers. Her pulse screamed in response.

He placed a hand at the base of her neck. "No peeking. Get comfortable."

She wanted to ask why but also wanted to be surprised. She folded her arms and rested her chin on them. "Done."

"There's a part of me that's jealous about the bottle of lavender massage oil in the bathroom." A soft pop filled the room. A lid being opened for the first time? "But it's tempered by the fact you've never used it."

"It was a white elephant gift."

"Lucky me." The faint scent of lavender drifted through the air. Seconds later, his hands found her shoulders.

The touch was enough to drive her wild, but when he began to massage, grip sliding easily with the help of the oil, her tension faded away. She moaned softly each time he hit a tight muscle.

"You need to learn to unwind."

"Whatever you say." She had zero desire to argue.

He worked his way along her neck and shoulders, rubbing and forcing away the knots, spending several minutes in each spot before moving to the next. Relaxation forced aside her pent up stress…concerns…fears…everything.

He reached her lower back, and she gasped at the bunched up muscles he dug his thumbs into.

"Too much?" His attentions slowed.

"No." She shook her head. "Perfect. Don't stop."

"I like the way you say that." He worked deeper into the tissue, working the area until it was hot.

His hands slid over her ass, and she let out a soft giggle at the light touch. When he reached her thighs, she sighed. He paid as much attention there, and then to her calves and feet, as he had everywhere else.

Her entire body was tingling when he finally broke away, and her eyelids were threatening to droop shut.

He crawled up the bed next to her and lay on his back. She shifted her position, so she could rest her head on his shoulder and her hand on his chest.

"You're not coming back to Salt Lake, are you?" He rested his hand on her hip.

She'd missed this closeness so much, and it ached to give him an honest answer. "I'm still under contract here, and your numbers…"

He sighed. "I know. They don't add up."

Maybe it was a good thing they didn't fuck. It was already going to hurt to say goodbye in the morning. "If I could see any way…"

"Yeah. Me too."

A heavy silence fell between them.

Rae traced lines over Zach's bare chest, listening to the soft beat of his heart. She needed to burn this moment in her mind forever. She didn't know when she was going to get a chance to relive it. She looked around her bedroom as much as she could without moving. The flower prints on the walls. The comforter and sheets in a color scheme that matched the taupe paint. Or was it beige? It made her a little sad she'd never decorated the room to reflect her personality.

"What are you thinking about?"

His soft question startled her, but there was no reason to hide anymore. "How much I'm going to miss you."

He pulled her closer. "If I thought even for a minute it wouldn't make you completely miserable, I'd ask you to quit and just come stay with me. I could take care of us both." A deep tremor ran through his voice.

Her chest ached. They both knew neither of them would be happy like that. "If you're good—like really, really good—even if, for some strange reason, the response at E3 is only lukewarm, you can stay solvent until you start turning a profit. That means a hiring freeze and minimal pay raises."

"You say the sexiest things in bed."

"I can't help it. I don't want to watch you leave again, and I can't think of a way to change it."

"Technically, I didn't leave last time, so I can't leave again."

She shook her head without lifting it. "I still wish there was another way."

"Me too. Are you coming back to Salt Lake after your contract is up?"

She bit the inside of her cheek. "I don't know." She'd considered it, but shot the idea down as false home so many times, she learned to ignore it before it even became a fully-formed thought.

"You won't cut me off though, right?" There was a trace of hesitation in his question she didn't think she'd ever heard before. "We'll still do this long distance?"

She nodded against his skin. "You couldn't stop me."

chapter twenty-two

Nervous energy thrummed through Zach. He tapped his foot against the concrete and checked his watch again.

Chloe hopped onto a nearby stool, feet swinging back and forth. "That doesn't make the time go any faster, you know."

"I know." As much as he was grateful to have her assistance, he couldn't help wishing Rae were there instead. And he had no idea how Chloe was so calm.

Scott sat on a second stool behind the tall table they'd set their demo stations up on. He stretched and popped his neck. His shirt matched Chloe's. White, obnoxious logo stretched across the front, but about three sizes bigger. "You know it's too late to worry, right? I mean, either it goes well now or it doesn't. Besides, it's not like anyone's going to be this far back in the room when the doors open."

"You're not helping." Zach couldn't keep his expression stern long enough for it to make an impact. His clothing matched theirs. He couldn't believe they had talked him into the casual outfits. It was an industry affair. He should be in a suit and tie.

He should be mingling. He should be headlining the large Cord/DM booth positioned directly in front of the entrance to the exhibitors' hall instead of hidden in a corner like a nobody.

That was a bad road to go down. He was over that need. But part of him still remembered the attention they'd drawn two years before. The memory brought back another, more bitter one— Kelly turning down his marriage proposal in front of thousands during their game launch. On second thought, he was definitely better off tucked out of sight with his friends.

Chloe moved from one demo station to the next, loading up the game on each. "We'll be fine. Amazing even. You have a good team."

Scott cleared his throat. "And they're so modest, too."

She glanced over her shoulder but didn't stop working. "I learned it from the best."

Scott laughed. "Flattery still doesn't lead to raises."

She looked at Zach. "That's not what you told me."

Zach shook his head, the banter pushing aside some of his tension. "Bullshit, it's not."

"Psst." A stage whisper interrupted.

The three of them turned in unison.

Jordan stood at the edge of the booth, DM button-down tucked into beige slacks. "Hey, guys."

"Hey, traitor." Chloe winked at him. She stepped forward and straightened his collar. "You look like a proper corporate tool."

Jordan rolled his eyes and grabbed his crotch.

"I've got your corporate tool right here. What you have is amazing, right?"

Scott tossed him a shrink-wrapped demo disc. "Like you haven't seen it already. Had to get some old-school hack to build the engine."

Jordan snagged the square out of the air. He studied the package, smirking. "I'm sure you did fine. You even rocked the artwork. And the logo." His gaze fell to Chloe's chest. "Definitely rocked the logo."

She snapped her fingers in front of his face. "Are you allowed to be over here?"

Jordan smirked and took a step forward. He whispered something in her ear.

Chloe snorted with laughter. "Still looking forward to it."

He nodded. "You didn't tell, right?"

"Of course not."

He handed her the demo disc. "I've got a copy on my laptop. I probably shouldn't let them see me with it."

Zach sighed, not surprised. Even when Jordan hadn't had friends on the inside, back before Cord hired him, he hadn't had a problem getting his hands on pre-release demos of their games. Zach waited until Jordan was gone. "What are you two up to?"

Chloe didn't look at him, hands shoved in her pockets. "I'm not allowed to tell. Don't worry; it's not bad."

"Not reassuring." Scott's comment echoed Zach's sentiments. "It's ten, by the way. Doors are opening."

The earlier nervousness returned, pulsing

through Zach's veins and sitting heavy in his stomach. He pasted a smile on and paced to the edge of the booth, watching the media and attendees spill into the exhibit hall.

And they waited. The minutes became hours. The occasional person came by and grabbed a demo disc off the stack, but didn't make eye contact with any of them.

Chloe sighed and leaned back against a nearby table, hands in her pockets. "How much longer till the courtesy suites open?"

Zach rolled his eyes. "One: no courtesy suites. Rae will kill me if I let you get drunk. And two: it's barely noon."

Chloe scrunched up her face. "Great. Now I have a babysitter."

Maybe mentioning Rae had been a bad idea. A whisper of longing floated through him. It didn't feel right with her not there. Even if he didn't miss her so much, she'd earned it as much as any of them.

"Excuse me." A smooth tenor interrupted the light-hearted exchange. "I'm looking for a Scott McAllister or a Zach Johnston?"

Zach started to correct the older gentleman out of habit—except he'd pronounced Zach's last name right. Nice change. He extended his hand. "I'm Zach." And nodded to his left. "This is Scott."

"Gentlemen." The new arrival was about the same build as Zach and wore a tailored suit—silk probably—complete with cuff links and topped off with a leather briefcase. He shook everyone's hands. "Grant Lent. I've heard a lot about you."

Zach's smile froze. That never meant good

things. And why did that name sound familiar? "I'd like to say the same."

Grant gave a deep chuckle. "Do the two of you have a moment?"

"Sure. Step into our private office." Sarcasm traced Scott's reply, and he nodded to the empty space behind the wall of their booth.

If the tone bothered Grant, it didn't show. His wide smile never wavered. "I won't take you away for long." The three of them crossed the short distance to out of sight. "I hear you have fantastic things on the horizon."

Zach bit back the question on the tip of his tongue.

Scott didn't. "Who told you that?"

Zach wanted to be bothered by the blunt approach, but at least it might mean an answer.

Grant shook his head. "The word is out, here and there. Thing is, I like what I've seen, and I'm impressed you've done so much with so little." He pulled a card from his shirt pocket and handed it to Zach. "And I want in on the ground floor."

No way. That's why Zach knew the name. Grant owned one of the largest private investment groups in the country. He pocketed the card. He didn't want to say this, but continuing the conversation would be a mistake.

"I'm sorry." Scott spoke up first. "We're not looking for funding. Whatever you heard must be skewed."

Zach bit the inside of his cheek. He might not have been able to turn it down so easily. He wasn't sure if that was a good thing or bad.

Grant didn't flinch. "Completely understand. If anything changes in the future, hold onto my card."

This was too easy. This man was amicable, polite, and hadn't once talked down to them. Zach was starting to feel comfortable around him, and that made him nervous.

"Humor me, though," Grant said. "If we're not talking money, pretend I'm like anyone else you'll meet today. My grandson loves these games. Tell me why he should play yours."

"Because it's awesomely unlike anything out there." Scott didn't miss a beat.

Zach shrugged. "Not how I would have put it, but pretty much."

As the conversation shifted from one topic to another, Zach realized he and Scott were both getting along splendidly with Grant. It was the first time he could remember at one of these shows where he'd actually enjoyed a conversation with a suit instead of just chiseling on a smile to make it through the day. It felt good.

"Sorry to interrupt" —Chloe poked her head around the corner— "but we're kind of slammed out here. You know, if you've got a minute or two?"

"I'll let you go." Grant shook their hands again, already stepping away. "My grandson will be thrilled to know I met you, and you aren't assholes."

Zach couldn't help but laugh at the parting words. His smile was still genuine as they rounded the corner. And then he paused, eyes growing wide. Chloe hadn't been kidding. Every single demo station was filled, and lines were forming. She was fielding questions left and right.

Two more guys approached, demo discs in hand.

"Hey, she was right." The skinny one took his place in one of the demo lines.

"You guys really helped write the original Legion?" the larger one asked Chloe.

"Helped, yeah." Scott's response was flat. He didn't have time to get into it, as a girl approached. And then a group of three. And then someone wearing a press pass for an online review site.

They spent the next half hour answering questions, giving demos, and making small talk with the sudden onset of people. Zach engaged a couple of visitors in conversation and managed to learn that the flirty girl Rinslet gave the shirt to was talking them up and handing out discs.

He grabbed Chloe. "You've been here the whole time, right?"

Chloe stared back, mouth twisted, brows raised.

"Right. I know." Of course she had. Zach shook his head. "Then who are they talking about? Who else has one of our shirts?"

Chloe turned away from his gaze. "I might have given one to Jordan. He is kind of pretty."

A whisper echoed in the back of Zach's head, and he ignored it. Pretending even for a second Rae was there would get him in trouble. Still, what was Chloe keeping from him? He grabbed Scott's attention away from a blogger asking intense questions about their coding methodology. "Hey, I'm gonna go find us some lunch. Will you be okay for a few minutes?"

Scott pursed his lips. "Five, tops."

"I promise." Zach extracted himself from the crowd. They needed to eat, but food was just an excuse. Too much was happening. He needed to walk away, clear his head, and convince the nagging part of his brain that wouldn't shut up that Rae was nowhere in the building.

Seven minutes later, over-priced hot dogs and drinks in hand, he returned to the finally ebbing flow of interest. Of course he hadn't seen her. Because she wasn't there. So why wouldn't the hopeful and suspicious part of his brain shut up?

chapter twenty-three

Zach slid into the back of the auditorium next to his friends. He didn't want to be there. He wanted to be as far away as possible. The thought made his feet twitch, and he tapped his toes to keep from indulging in the compulsion. He would have settled for drinking in the hotel bar, but Chloe had insisted they needed to attend this. She said it would give them closure.

The same sick feeling churned in his gut that had been there two years ago. Except then it had been because he was planning to propose to Kelly to launch their new game. This time it was because someone else was launching their game, and their names wouldn't be anywhere on it.

"Hold still," Scott growled.

Zach knew he was in trouble if Scott was complaining about him fidgeting. Zach clamped his jaw shut and folded his arms. He leaned against the back wall, hiding in the shadows and trying to calm down. It didn't help.

Chloe stood a few feet from both of them, feet shuffling back and forth. "It'll be fine."

"How can you promise that?" Scott asked.

"Because I'm not the one with bad memories attached to that stage." She nodded toward the front of the room.

That wasn't helpful.

Jordan stepped on the stage, and the audience erupted in cheers.

"DM let him do this?" Scott asked.

"He's their rebel poster boy," Zach replied, voice low. Something about this felt wrong. It was just his imagination, right? Bad memories were making him paranoid. "Of course they did."

"Good evening, Los Angeles." Jordan's voice carried through the crowd. "I hear you're here to see something epic."

More applause rolled through the room, punctuated with a few yells and whistles.

An ache hammered in Zach's skull. The whole thing was too familiar. Even the working of the crowd was almost identical to two years ago.

Chloe moved farther away. "Try not to throw up before this is all over."

That wasn't helpful either.

"You're going to have to wait just a little longer," Jordan continued.

"What the hell?" Scott straightened up, echoing Zach's thoughts.

A hush fell over the audience.

"There's a special young lady in the audience this evening." Jordan stepped away from the podium.

The speech wasn't just similar to two years ago—it was identical to Zach's.

"What the fuck is he doing?" Scott looked at Zach.

Zach frowned. "No clue."

Chloe was gone, vanished out a side door without another comment.

"Chloe, sweetheart, are you out there?" Jordan called into the dark auditorium.

Scott coughed.

"What?" Zach asked. They couldn't be doing this.

Except a familiar head of black hair had emerged from the audience and was walking toward the stage.

Jordan kept talking. "You have to understand, this woman is amazing. She's the reason I can wake up in the morning, and the reason I can do what I'm doing today."

Zach was going to be ill, he knew it. This wasn't funny. He could tell from Scott's expression he was in agreement. Murmurs spread across the crowds, as others started to draw the same connection to what was happening.

Chloe stepped onto the stage, and Jordan walked to meet her. He took her hand and led her into the spotlight. Coming to a stop, he kissed her on the cheek. He dropped to one knee, and the quiet roar in the audience increased several decibels. He kept going. "Chloe, you've been a constant source of light in my life since I met you. You've shown me opportunities I never imagined existed."

Zach wanted to turn away, but his gaze was fixed on the stage. Morbid fascination threatened to make him lose his lunch.

"I know this is sudden, but I was wondering, would you do me the honor of becoming my wife?"

"Fuck me," Scott muttered. "I'm going to kill him with my own hands. I don't care if the entire internet sees it."

Zach placed a restraining hand on his arm, not trusting himself to speak.

Chloe shook her head and broke away. "I don't think so. I mean, really. Who wants to be married to a game programmer?"

And Zach's heart sank further. The déjà vu was painful. The success of the last forty-eight hours was evaporating.

But where Kelly's no had stopped there, Chloe's didn't. "I mean one that works for Digital Media, anyway. *Eww.* Is it true they pay you monkeys in bananas?"

Scott's eyes grew wide. "Did she just…really?"

This was going to cause them so much trouble. There was no way anyone would believe they hadn't set the whole thing up.

Jordan sniffled into the microphone, expression flat. "Peanuts, actually."

Chloe pulled him to his feet and stepped closer to drape her arms around his neck. "I can make you a better offer."

Something caught Zach's attention, and he realized the media reps for DM were standing off stage, fighting desperately to get Jordan's attention. Cameras turned toward the new commotion.

Jordan smirked and leaned into her. "Really? Better than peanuts?"

She leaned forward, whispering right next to his mike. "Ditch the losers, and I'm all yours."

Jordan stepped away, grinning.

The media reps had given up trying to catch his attention and were converging on the center stage.

Zach felt relief wash over him. He couldn't believe what he was seeing.

Scott was laughing. "Holy fuck. I can't believe he put her up to this."

Someone grabbed Jordan's arm at the same time as another person took hold of Chloe. Vance stepped up to the mike, laughing nervously. The lights exaggerated the sweat dripping down his red face. "Very clever. Thank you, Jordan. Who wants to see our new game?"

The crowd wasn't listening. Attention was focused on the scuffle off-stage. Jordan's microphone was gone, so no sound filtered through the room, but he was gesturing wildly to the cronies accosting him. He yanked away from the one holding his arm and grabbed Chloe's hand. He said something else and tugged her toward the back exit.

Scott nudged Zach with his shoulder. "We should probably make ourselves scarce, no?"

Be furious or laugh? Zach wasn't sure which he wanted to do first. "We should take care of our people. You find them and keep them off the radar for a few hours. Lock them both in your room if you have to."

He stopped short of reaching for his smokes. That would have to wait. "I'm going to get a hold of marketing, see if we need to do damage control and how much, and put Legal on standby. Don't let them make it worse."

"Got it." Scott was already tapping on the screen of his phone as he walked away.

Zach took off in a different direction, looking for a quiet corner to start making phone calls. His phone vibrated in his pocket. Vance. Great. That voice mail could wait. This was insane. How were they going to convince the press—or even better, any furious lawyers—they hadn't known about this? He needed to get his people ready for damage control, depending on how the entire thing spun.

"I know you're busy, but do you have ten minutes for a friend?" The familiar female voice from somewhere to his right muted most of his other thoughts.

Rae. His already racing pulse kicked up another gear.

He whirled to find her lounging in the doorway of a dark conference room, a hesitant smile dancing on her lips. She looked incredible. She wore one of their shirts, and it hugged every inch of her torso as if it had been made for her. He couldn't find any words.

In a few short strides, he crossed the distance between them, wrapped an arm around her waist, and pulled her completely into the room, out of sight of foot traffic. He dipped his head and kissed her hard, hands sliding under her top and up her bare back, holding her as close as he could. Every inch of her rubbed against him. Her hands rested on his chest, a tiny whimper rising from her throat.

He finally broke the kiss with a gasp, but didn't let her go. "Did you know about any of this?"

She smirked. "Of course not. What my sister does in her spare time is completely up to her. It's called plausible deniability."

"You're so much trouble when I leave you alone."

"Then don't leave me alone." She rested her forehead against his chest, muffling her reply. "Besides, you know you love it."

"No. I love *you*." He kissed the top of her head. "The surprise in the DM presentation? I'm not sure I'm fond of."

She stepped back, putting enough space between them, so she could look him in the eye but not break his grip. She plucked something from her pocket and held it up between her thumb and forefinger. "Hopefully this will help."

He reluctantly let go of her to take the USB drive. "Naughty pictures?"

She shook her head, smile never leaving her face. "Three things, and that's not any of them."

Curiosity tried to worm its way into his already heavy onslaught of emotions. It wasn't easy, given the nagging voice reminding him people were probably really pissed about Chloe and Jordan's gimmick in the DM panel.

Even though he didn't want to admit it out loud, that single stunt had mocked his failed marriage proposal, reminded him things were a lot better now, and made DM look as bad now as he had back then. It would speak to fans and the media—anyone who remembered the original viral video. If he hadn't been worried about the consequences, he'd have a hard time complaining about the entire thing.

And he definitely wasn't complaining every time Rae's hip rubbed against him. His cock wanted him to forget everything but finishing what the kiss had started.

"Do tell." He forced the words out. He could do normal conversation for at least a couple more minutes. She was going to make it hard to focus on damage control.

"First." She leaned back against the wall, hooked her fingers in his front pockets, and drew him closer. "An investor agreement that keeps you both in complete control. Grant Lent, who I believe you met earlier, is very interested in the details."

Investors. The thought made his head throb. They needed the money, but at the same time, the idea of outside voices didn't sit well with him. "Okay?"

She brushed her lips over his. "Just give it a look. Second is solid, hardcore evidence that DM knew what Kelly was up to with the whole insider-trading thing, and they helped her figure out the details. Use it as leverage or however you see fit."

Oh, that was big. He'd always suspected—it was difficult not to—but to be able to prove it... There was a lot of potential there.

She kissed him again, more deeply this time, nipping at his bottom lip before pulling away. "So forgive me, maybe?"

She knew exactly how to distract him, but he'd been paying attention. "Maybe. Depends on what item number three is."

She traced a line down his chest. "Chloe and Jordan are with Scott. A press release is going out now about how the two of you knew nothing about this and, while it was funny as hell, you don't condone the action."

He tucked a strand of hair behind her ear, forcing his expression to stay serious. "Which makes it harder to believe you didn't know about this. And that means a press release isn't the third item on the drive."

Her flush was visible even in the poor lighting, and she ducked her head. Her reply was soft. "It's an employment agreement for your new CFO. If you decide to talk to Grant and the people he knows, you can afford it. Along with other people, like Jordan. We found a way around his contract."

She meant her. His heart leapt. "Presumptuous much?" The question didn't have any force behind it.

"Hopeful." She shuffled from one foot to the other. "Very, very hopeful."

"You should have told me what you were up to." Why was he still fighting this?

"I couldn't," she said. "You have to be able to honestly say you didn't know what we were doing."

She was good. And severely pushing the limits of his self-control. "So you're back for good?"

She shifted her weight against him, pulling him closer. "Most likely. It's not all up to me. But I love you, and I'm not ready to leave again. Beyond that, my staying means all involved parties are on board."

Love. The word stole his reason and floated through him on a thrum of desire. "In that case, welcome home." A new tension thrummed through him, heavy and anxious and having everything to do with the soft curves pressed against him. "Any plans this afternoon?"

"I was kind of hoping you were available."

"Only kind of?"

She slipped a finger inside the waist of his jeans and slid it across his bare stomach. "What do you think?"

What do I think? That he was seconds from pinning her to the wall and finding out just how far out of the line of traffic they were. "Tell me you know somewhere no one will find us or bother us for the rest of the night."

She laughed. "It's only five-thirty."

He nipped her shoulder with his teeth. "Good. Then we have plenty of time. Can you think of a better way to lie low?"

chapter twenty-four

She was back, she was his, and he was going to do everything in his power to make sure she didn't leave again.

Zach pulled Rae down next to him on the hotel bed. No one knew her name, so no one would be knocking on her door, asking about the stunt on stage. With any luck, he really could occupy her the rest of the night.

She tucked her legs under her, leaned forward, and then brushed her lips over his. The faint scent of strawberry combined with the taste of her kisses obliterated his control. He caught a fistful of her hair and tugged. She tilted her head back with a gasp, elongating her neck.

He ran his tongue up the tender skin, blood hot, cock already straining against his jeans. "Here's the thing." He couldn't keep the gravel from his voice. "You've dominated my fantasies for more than a year. I'm not going to be so great at taking this slow."

She hopped from the bed and scooted out of reach until she stood a few feet back, one corner of her mouth pulling up. "Then I guess you don't get to control how fast we go."

He grabbed for her, and she took another step back. *Fuck,* he wanted her. And yet part of him was intrigued to see what she was up to. "I'll play. For now."

She winked and kicked her shoes aside. Hips swaying as she danced in place to a tune only she could hear, she ran her hands down her sides. She grabbed the bottom of her shirt, still moving to a silent song. God, that was seductive. He leaned back on his hands, watching the show and trying to ignore the throb of need straining to get out of his jeans.

She took her shirt off and tossed it aside. Fuchsia bra. Nice. Her hands glided down her stomach and back up in a lazy spiral. She cupped her breasts through the fabric, eyelids fluttering as she caressed herself.

Spinning so her back was to him, she unhooked her bra. It slid down her arms and joined her top in a pile in the corner. She twirled back to face him, palms on her tits, rolling her nipples between her fingers.

This was getting painful, and he was loving the hell out of it. She stepped back to the bed, eyes narrowing when his hands came off the mattress. "Not yet," she warned.

His argument died in the back of his throat when she leaned over him and rested one hand on his upper thigh. She stroked the inside of his leg with her thumb, while seeking out his zipper with her other hand.

He groaned involuntarily when she slid his zipper down, and then wrapped her hand around his cock and freed it. She lowered her mouth until it was right next to his ear. "Your hands can do whatever they want to you," she whispered. "But keep in mind, I want to feel you inside me."

His heart hammered in his chest. He took his dick in his hand, making sure not to stroke too fast when she stepped away again. It wasn't the same anyway.

She went back to her slow dance. Hips always moving, her hands slid back down her sides and undid her own jeans but didn't strip them off.

She dipped her hand lower, sighing softly as her fingers disappeared inside her panties.

He wanted to be doing that. He couldn't peel his gaze from the show. He swore he was about to come when she raised two glistening fingers to her mouth and ran her tongue over them. She hooked her thumbs in her bottoms and pushed the rest of her clothes to the ground. He growled.

She dipped her fingers between her folds again, slowly stroking for a moment before moving toward him. The moment she was within reach, he grabbed her wrist and pulled her in the rest of the way. He placed one of her fingers in his mouth, ran his tongue along the pad, and sucked it clean, before moving to the other.

Her laughter died in a long groan. She nudged his shoulder with her free hand until he fell back. She straddled his legs but didn't lower herself. She dropped her head next to his ear again. "Here's the thing." Her voice was breathy and low. "I'm on birth control, and I trust you when you say you're clean. I don't think I want to do this whole *protection* thing anymore, but you have to be good with it too."

No condoms. For the first time since ever, that sounded appealing for more than just physical reasons. He grabbed her hips and brought her closer. "Sounds fantastic to me."

She lowered herself until her opening rested on the head of his cock. Wincing and gasping, she dropped lower and drove him deep inside. She sat straight up.

That was incredible. He pumped against her as she rode him, his hands on her thighs. The teasing had been almost as harsh as the last year of waiting though. He couldn't hold out much longer.

He moved one hand higher, thumb easily sliding between her slick lips and searching out her clit. She increased her rhythm as he stroked her swollen sex. Her short pants for breath matched his. She closed her eyes and tilted her head back, her cries echoing through the small room.

He'd missed that sound. It acted like a trigger, and he came inside her, pounding hard until he was spent.

The frantic pace slowed and then came to a stop. She leaned forward, resting against his chest. He wrapped his arms around her, holding her as close as he could. He was definitely doing everything in his power to make sure she didn't have to leave again.

Rae pressed into the warm body behind her. She'd missed so much about Zach, and waking up next to him was even more comforting than she remembered.

He didn't stir, and his steady breathing warmed the back of her neck. The clock said it was seven. He had to be up soon to make it to the exhibitor hall, so there was no point in her going back to sleep, but she also wasn't ready to get up.

She grabbed her phone off the nightstand instead, careful not to jostle him. Time to see what the fallout from yesterday looked like. She prayed she'd made the right call.

Her smile grew as she scanned industry headlines, E3 hashtags, and forums. DM was taking serious heat for the stunt. People were talking about how their arrogance was catching up to them. And about the old-newcomers who had owned the big boys and put DM in their place.

Lips glided along the back of her neck, sending a pleasant chill through her.

"They really like us, huh?" Zach's soft voice caressed her skin.

She set her phone aside, leaning more weight against him. "How much did you read?"

"Enough. Your shoulder was in the way of some of it." His palm rested on her stomach, holding her close. "We're lucky it didn't take a different turn. It might not have gone so well."

"True. But since it did, we're not dwelling. Besides, you built your career on being high risk."

"Hmm." Every time he spoke, it rumbled through her back. "Fair enough."

He was growing hard against her ass, and she pressed into his cock. "What time do you have to be downstairs?"

His hand slid up her chest, cupped one breast,

and then tweaked her nipple. He kissed along her shoulder. "Too soon."

She frowned, even though he couldn't see it. "We can be quick."

He rolled away and pulled her onto her back. Seconds later, he was straddling her, gaze tracing her face. "It's tempting." He placed his hands on the bed, on either side of her head, and kissed her. "You're tempting." His mouth moved along her jaw. "But I have to do something first, and it's important, and I promise if it goes well I'm all yours in my free time."

She tried to smile. Of course business still came first. She knew that. "I'll let you get to it then."

He rolled off her, grabbed her hands, and helped her sit up across from him. "How much longer are you in town?"

"Until the end of the show. Like I said last night, I was hopeful."

He grinned. "God, I love you."

The words warmed her and tempered her disappointment, even though they didn't erase it.

"Here's the thing," he continued before she could respond. "We're doing a live demo this afternoon."

"All right?"

"And it's going to be hard to top what happened to DM yesterday, but I'd like to at least make a splash."

"Which you will. Your game is brilliant." He wanted his ego stroked? That didn't make any sense. She was missing something.

"And I was thinking maybe we could announce we have a new CFO—maybe turn some heads by bringing you up on stage?"

She laughed and ducked her head, heat flooding her cheeks. "I hardly think I'm media worthy."

He placed a finger under her chin and raised her face again. "It worked yesterday. Is that a yes?"

"Absolutely." Giddiness floated through her. They were going to bring her on after all. She hadn't realized how much she'd missed the idea, but knowing she could have that back—a solid job with a company she actually believed in—filled her with all sorts of happy thoughts.

"That was easier than I thought." His laugh was nervous. "Next one is a bit harder for me."

"Oh?" She leaned closer, curious.

He rested his hands on her cheeks, holding her gaze. "Where are you staying when you move back?"

"Chloe's guest room or some long-term motel until I find a new place. I'll figure it out." She had a couple of options, but hadn't wanted to set anything in stone until she knew the company would take her back.

"With me?"

She blinked as the words sank in. "As in, long term?"

He kissed her deeply, holding her face, hunger and need on his lips. She gasped when they broke apart. That sensation was still incredible.

He didn't let go. "As in long term. Move in with me?"

She should think about it. It was such a rash decision to make given how much planning had gone into everything else. "Okay." Her mouth stole hesitation from her. As soon as she agreed, she knew it was exactly what she wanted. "Yes. I'd love to."

He kissed her quickly again and then climbed to his feet, tugging her after him. "Good. We should get downstairs."

She draped her hands at the base of his neck, fingers interlocked, and drew his head down. She pressed her lips to his and then darted her tongue in his mouth, as her entire body rubbed against his bare skin.

She was breathless when they broke apart. "I guess. But you owe me later."

"Without question. I'm so glad you're back."

"Me too." She felt lighter than she had in a year.

He slid a hand down her back, over her ass, and then between her legs. "Maybe we can take a little longer in the shower before we make our entrance."

She kissed him again, pressing close, growing wet at the hard arousal digging into her stomach. "I'm in."

The End

Scott's story is available in *His Reputation*. Keep reading for a sneak peek of chapter one

his reputation

chapter one

There were times when Kenzie envied her sister's ability to slide into new relationships. Admired the way Riley always found the guys who knew how to have fun. Wished she could let loose like her twin.

Her envy tended to evaporate when Riley showed up on her doorstep at midnight—the way she had last night—cheeks smeared with tears and mascara, bags in hand and looking for a place to crash.

Kenzie inched forward with the line in the coffee shop, focused more on her thoughts than the Saturday morning crowds pushing in on her. Once she had her tea, she could concentrate on all the ways her love life wasn't pathetic. First way was… *Nope, total blank.*

Okay, that was a failed exercise.

An hour ago Kenzie had tried to dig for more information. To help. To nudge Riley into spilling what had gone wrong and maybe offer a little advice in return. Her reward? Insults.

Riley's words echoed in Kenzie's thoughts, taunting her in rhythm with the chatter of people around her. Kenzie wasn't frigid. She'd been the one to leave her last boyfriend for not delivering on the excitement in the bedroom. Just because she was picky about the men she dated didn't mean she was uptight. Refusing to go out with anyone who thought chartreuse was a flavor of frozen yogurt didn't make her a bad person.

And preferring her men clean and publicly presentable didn't mean she lacked imagination.

When Kenzie reached the front counter, glass cases filled with pastries mocked her. The plum tarts looked good, but indulging a sugar craving wasn't the way to sate her wounded ego. She ordered a large peppermint tea. The room dimmed as clouds outside drifted in front of the sun.

She grabbed her drink and scanned the crowded room for a place to sit and sip. Not a single unoccupied table, but three had available seats. A woman sat at the first, trying to force-feed the baby in her lap a pacifier while Mom sucked on a latte. At the second, two teenage boys stared at their phones, their only verbal conversation the occasional laughter as they smacked each other on the arm.

Then there was the scenery at table three.

The man with a shock of brown, spiked hair, broad shoulders, and a tattered T-shirt that looked like it had seen one too many accidental bleachings dominated a table in the corner of the room, one of the few empty chairs next to him. The clothes made him look twenty, but he held himself with a confidence that made her think he was actually older than her twenty-six.

She had no idea who he was, but she saw him almost every weekend, and used the fact he was frequently engrossed in something on his phone or some game device as an excuse to study him without getting caught staring.

What's keeping you from approaching him? The question taunted her in Riley's voice. It wasn't as if she was shy.

The answer was painfully obvious. *It's not appropriate.* Women didn't hit on random men in coffee shops.

Riley would. Hell, Riley would have had his number weeks ago, and probably been living with him just a few days later.

Kenzie took a deep breath. She could at least strike up a conversation and see where things went from there. She approached the empty spot before she could talk herself out of it, and forced confidence into her voice. "Excuse me."

"Hmm?" He barely moved his head, immersed in something on his phone.

"Is this seat taken?"

He pulled his attention from the screen long enough to rake his gaze over her. Her breath caught at the deep brown of his eyes. *Gorgeous.* Just as quickly, he turned back to his phone. A flicker of a smile tugged up the corner of his mouth. "It's not taken yet, but I'm hoping you'll have a seat and solve that problem."

What now? She'd never played the role of aggressor before, but she was already realizing it was easier to be the one doing the turning down than the one doing the asking.

"Do you come here often?" She winced at the pathetic line the moment it was out.

He spared her another glance, laughter dancing on his face. "Probably at least as often as you."

And that was it. He was buried in his distraction again.

How embarrassing. She exhaled. This wasn't worth the effort, but it would look awkward if she left so soon. She should at least use the seat she'd secured. Grabbing her phone, she pulled up the book she'd been in the middle of and tried to lose herself in the pages while she drank her tea.

Background noise screamed around her, and she pushed it aside. A creeping heat flooded her face as something tickled her senses. Was someone watching her? She looked up, startled to see the man across from her glancing between the phone and her.

She shifted her attention from her book—Scott assumed it was a book since she was staring at a white screen with lots of black letters. Her piercing blue eyes were curious, and a hard line disrupted the swelling in her flushed lips. It was time to forget the game he was testing for work.

He'd noticed her before. The long legs, narrow waist, and round ass accentuated her jeans the way the over-priced designer had intended, and the entire package was always nice to look at. But the fact that her wardrobe screamed *I don't mind overpaying for a label* reminded him of too many women he dated who preferred his wallet to his company.

"Is something wrong?" She stared back, face quirked in question.

He'd been surprised and curious when she approached, and amused by the hesitation coming from a woman who held herself with so much confidence. It was a shame she let the conversation die when he went to save his game, and he was hoping to reinitiate it. Find out more about this potential dichotomy.

"Nothing's wrong." He met her steady gaze, keeping his tone even but not able to hide all his amusement. "Just wondering something."

She ducked her head, gaze falling to his hand before it quickly jumped back to his face. "What's that?"

The flush on her cheeks was enticing. How much redder could he make her go before she slapped him? Or let him brush his mouth over hers. He nodded at her phone. "How contrived their happily ever after is."

"Excuse me?"

Yup, she was going to slap him. Or at least grind her heel into his toes. Thank the open-source gods she wore sneakers and not heels.

"The big tough hero and his dainty mistress." He knew better than to assume, but that had never stopped him in the past, and everything about her, from the way she'd folded a napkin on her knee to the ponytail that didn't look like it would budge even with a solid, impassioned tug, screamed repressed. "Is he a duke? Or maybe she's a stripper with a heart of gold?" One of his two best friends, Rae, was forever losing herself in romance novels. He adored her, but never understood her fascination with the books. Reality wasn't happily ever after.

His tablemate rolled her eyes and slid the phone across the table. "*He's* a teenager who was psychologically tortured by Homeland Security for more than a week, and *she's* helping him get back at *the man.*"

That sounded familiar. He tapped the screen to bring up the book information. *Little Brother*. His smile turned genuine. "My mistake. Good book, I won't spoil the ending."

The ambivalence in her half-formed smile stole his next breath. Her tone was dry. "I appreciate it. Sorry to disappoint you, but bad euphemisms aren't my thing."

This was fun. "Really? Sacred vees and turgid manhood—or is it manhoods, plural? Or maybe that's a different kind of story. That doesn't do anything for you?"

She dropped the phone into her purse, mouth still twitching in indecision. Damn that was a good look for her.

"Not on paper." She ran a tongue over her bottom lip before catching it between her teeth.

He wouldn't mind giving that a try. Nipping at that full almost-pout. His pulse sped up at the banter. He pushed his game aside and leaned in, fingers clasped and hands resting on the table. He was going to enjoy this for as long as she wanted to keep it up.

The last couple of women he'd been with—hell, even his last couple of girlfriends before that—had been more giggle than brain. Cared more about how they looked on his arm than what he had to say.

He was sick of fake girls only interested in his money. This woman though, she radiated intelligence, genuineness, and had no idea who he was. "They were wrong. It's not more fun than a gorgeous woman."

"They?" Her flush spread to her neck.

Long, slender. What would it be like to run his tongue along that slope? "Marketing. They're making promises they can't keep." He pushed his half-eaten donut aside. Her bold responses mingled with the hesitation and embarrassment, flushing her pale skin, and all of it short circuiting his thoughts. He wanted more. "So you'd rather the exploration of honeyed walls took place in real life."

Disbelief mingled with her laughter. "Are you always so forward?"

Frequently, to the dismay of his board of directors. Another shadow passed through the shop as clouds covered the sun outside for a moment. "Only until it gets me slapped. You?"

"Always and for as long as I can get away with it." She shifted in her seat, leaning in, arms resting on the table and accentuating full breasts.

He forced his attention to stay on her face. She wasn't even close to the prissy socialite he'd imagined. It had been a long time since he pegged someone so completely wrong, and he was enjoying the hell out of it.

Her phone interrupted, a tinny pop song cutting

through the veil of innuendo. She gave him an apologetic glance. "I'm sorry."

He waved a dismissive hand. "No worries. If it's your boyfriend asking you to talk dirty to him, go ahead."

"Not likely. No boyfriend." She answered the phone. "What? …I stopped for tea someplace where they weren't going to snap at me for being nice." She glanced at him, hesitation in her eyes, and then shook her head. "Fine, okay. I'll be back in a little bit."

She dropped her phone in her purse and turned to him. "I'd love to stay longer, talk about whether or not one's manhood can actually throb, but I have to go."

"Shame. I might have proposed a hands-on experiment." He shoved the rest of his donut in his mouth and washed it down with a swallow of coffee.

"Does talking like that ever get you in trouble?"

"Let's just say I'm willing to take my chances in some cases." He stood and offered her a hand. "I should probably get back to real life too. I'll walk you out."

His hand lingered on her arm as he guided her through the crowds toward the exit, her warm skin against his sending pulsing tingles through him. When they stepped onto the sidewalk, the din of Saturday morning traffic rushed in to replace the chatter of inside. "Where did you park?" He was pretty sure he'd never seen her drive—it was hard to miss those things on mornings when the place was deserted except for the two of them—but it was polite to ask.

"Home."

That was a more vague answer than he was looking for, but it wasn't as if he wanted to meet her family. Or her cats. Whatever. His hand moved to the small of her back, nudging her across the parking lot. She didn't resist.

"Do you want a lift?" he asked.

Her footsteps slowed, and she pulled away. "In the love van?"

He spun to face her, not sure what to make of the comment. She'd nicknamed his car? *Fascinating.* "Excuse me?"

She nodded at the Escalade in the back of the parking lot. "That one's yours right? The Game God license plate? The tinted windows meant to keep out even the most penetrating light?"

She knew what the G4M3G0D on his plates meant. She was full of entertaining surprises. He bit back the urge to joke about the word *penetrating.* "That's it, but love van, really?"

She fell into step beside him again. "I can't be the only person who's called it that."

"To my face at least. Interesting assumption." He moved closer, letting his bare arm brush hers.

"No worse than deciding I was reading some bodice ripper inside."

He stopped at his SUV, spinning to face her and leaning back against it, one foot propped up on the rubber strip running along the bottom of the door. He looped his thumbs in his pockets. "Fair enough. We're even on the inappropriate assumption front then?"

She kept her distance but didn't seem in a hurry to leave. "I didn't know we were keeping score."

A gust of wind tore through the parking lot and whipped her ponytail into her face. She hugged herself and shivered as the clouds devoured the last traces of direct sunlight.

He forced his hands to stay by his side, biting his tongue before he could offer to warm her up. Or ask if she'd like to be the one biting his tongue. "Someone's always keeping score."

"Clever." A sharp chill wove itself into the wind, and she rubbed the visible goose bumps on her arms. Even through her bra, he could see her nipples were hard nubs, adding new geography to her fitted T-shirt.

He shouldn't be staring. Or imagining pulling her close, running his hands over those peaks, warming her up. He clicked the locks off on his car, yanked the door open, and grabbed his jacket off the back seat.

"Hmm…" Her voice was closer than she expected. "Clean. Beige leather. No shag carpet." He turned and she stepped back, ducking her head. "I had to see for myself."

"Sorry to disappoint you." He draped the fleece over her shoulders, and pulled the neck closed, hands lingering on her collarbone. The soft fruit of her shampoo mingled with a flowered perfume. He pushed back the urge to pull her closer, breathe her in, and taste her.

"Not disappointed at all."

Even though she was only a few inches shorter than his six two, she almost swam in the coat, the bottom hanging halfway down her thighs. An image flashed through his mind of her wearing nothing but that jacket, standing in his bedroom doorway—

A sharp bolt lit up the sky, accompanied by the concussive boom of thunder. She jumped, eliminating a few more inches between them, and laughed nervously, hand flying to her chest. "Holy crap."

His heart was hammering too, but not from the sudden noise. She stood near enough her warmth drifted toward his bare arms. Her gaze met his, and his breath caught. Such a captivating face.

A drop of rain landed on her cheek, then trailed down the smooth skin. He rested a hand on the back of her neck, thumb brushing away the water. His pulse raced even faster when she tilted her head into the gesture.

Another drop landed on her nose, her forehead, her chin. What would she do if he kissed them away?

The sky opened up, buckets pouring down, plastering his shirt to him in seconds.

She pulled his jacket tighter. "I think I'll take that ride after all."

He didn't argue, yanking open the passenger door and making sure she was inside before sprinting to the driver's side.

The story continues on chapter two...